THE CASE OF
THE KIDNAPPED SHADOW
Thomas Brace Haughey

THE CASE OF
THE
KIDNAPPED
SHADOW

Thomas Brace Haughey

Bethany Fellowship INC.
MINNEAPOLIS, MINNESOTA 55438

Illustrations by Ken Lochhead

The Case of the Kidnapped Shadow
Thomas Brace Haughey

Library of Congress Catalog Card Number 80-65945

ISBN 0-87123-112-3

Published by Bethany Fellowship, Inc.
6820 Auto Club Road, Minneapolis, Minnesota 55438

Printed in the United States of America

Dedication

To Marta Rocha, Chris Thompson, and all the Harders, who nearly took the "hard" out of my stay in Mexico City. Thanks for the hospitality, subway tickets, and the loan of soft shoes for blistered feet.

About the Author

Thomas Brace Haughey is the General Director of The Evangelical Latin League mission and its branch, Fireside Productions. He is also involved in the work of missionary radio station KVMV-FM in McAllen, Texas. He received his bachelor's degree from the University of Maryland in 1965, and a Th.M. from Capital Bible Seminary in 1969. In addition, he received a diploma from Rio Grande Bible Institute Language School. While at the University of Maryland, he was inducted into the literary honorary society, Phi Delta Epsilon. He has done evangelism and youth work in Mexico, and taught for a year and a half in a missionary Bible school. His experience as a writer includes: Editing a Jesus Paper, writing numerous articles, writing scripts for "Folk Festival," a weekly radio program, and more than 100 book reviews each year for broadcast. Mr. Haughey is married, has one daughter, and makes his home in McAllen, Texas. This is his fourth book.

Preface

There is no such thing as a "typical" mystery writer. Each is unique. Robert Louis Stevenson, for example, was a cripple when he penned such stories as *The Dynamiter* and *The Wrong Box*. Charles Dickens, the son of a debtor's prison inmate, worked in sweat shops before gaining literary prominence and inventing Inspector Bucket—the first big English clue-scooper. Erle Stanley Gardner shifted from boxer, to fight promotor, to lawyer, and then flooded the pulp market with fiction. The aristocratic sportsman A. Conan Doyle served as a ship's doctor on an Arctic whaler and an African steamer, set up private practice in Portsmouth, and started writing between appointments.

As divergent as these gentlemen were, however, they shared a common zest for life. They cared enough to throw spectator tickets to the wind and get involved. Their writing reflected that attitude.

Detective story writers are an amazingly interesting lot. Like Dickens, they may be social critics. They are generally individualists. And a few—believe it or not—are actually amateur sleuths. Gardner helped found the Court of Last Resort to help wrongfully convicted felons.

Doyle, while not busy in Parliament, solved at least two notable cases. In one, he proved that George Edalji, son of a Staffordshire minister, had not maimed horses. The deduction freed the young man four years before completing his seven-year sentence. In the second, A. Conan rescued Oscar Slater from a successful jewel robbery frame-up. Slater won a resulting damage suit but neglected to reimburse the amateur detective for court costs.

In light of mystery writers' tendency toward involvement, it's natural to wonder just how much of their "fiction" is fiction. How much have they been influenced by their experiences? Is Sherlock Holmes based upon Dr. Joseph Bell, one of Doyle's professors at Edinburg University? Is Dr. Watson a doctor because Doyle was? Is Della Street a composite of Gardner's three secretaries?

I suspect that there's much to commend such theories. Only the Lord creates out of nothing. Mortals need at least a few points of reference in real life around which to weave plot and action.

Characters cry for sympathetic writers. Most probably, John Taylor picked me to record his partner's exploits for that very reason. Since I'm an evangelical, he knew he could trust me not to gloss over Geoffrey Weston's more theological debates. Or he may have simply felt that anyone shot at for preaching a sermon couldn't be all bad.

For whatever the reason, I've been selected. And I've found setting down *The Case of the Kidnapped Shadow* especially enjoyable. Perhaps that's because it contains an element of nostalgia for me.

Grandnephews sometimes turn out well. The Green Hornet, you'll remember, was a worthy successor to the Lone Ranger. And Geoffrey Weston in his latest adventure certainly shows all the dash, flair, and genius of his Great-uncle Sherlock. When faced with an impossible kidnapping, an unknown kidnappee, an entire government on the brink of toppling, and an attempt to destroy him, he reaches into his thinking cap for the proverbial conejo (rabbit).

If you enjoy surprise endings, I invite you to continue reading and to match wits with Geoff and his friend, John Taylor. While you're about it, you might ask yourself where fiction ends and fact begins.

Table of Contents

Chapter 1

The Information Gap

As the Concorde II began its descent, I set aside my copy of the London *Telegraph* and gazed idly out the window. Mexico City glittered below us like a constellation, sparkles strewn across an immense black bowl. Scattered amid the flecks, red and blue pinpoints beckoned insistently to the earthbound consumers. Even at three in the morning the city seemed to be bustling with activity. As we continued to lose altitude I could just make out the slender outline of the Latin American Tower thrusting skyward, half its windows still aglow. Then the jetliner banked steeply and everything but stars slid from view. A stewardess' crisp voice on the intercom brought my attention back to the dim interior of the cabin.

"We shall be landing in approximately six minutes. Please be sure your seats and trays are in an upright position. Be sure your seat belts are fastened, and please observe the no smoking signs."

Up and down the aisle other passengers were beginning the usual pre-landing activity. I gave my partner a gentle nudge with my elbow.

"You'd best pry your eyelids open, old bean. The bird's nose is drooping and we're starting our landing glide."

Geoffrey Weston groaned and grudgingly pressed the button that raised his recliner back to vertical.

"I hope," he remarked sleepily, "that we catch the proverbial worm." He fought off a yawn, rubbing his stubbled cheeks. "We're certainly up early enough."

"Not much doubt of that," I agreed. "Up in more ways than one. . ." He wasn't too sleepy to give me a pained look.

"But if that worm you're referring to is a kidnapper rather than some bug on the runway," I continued, ignoring his implicit sarcasm, "we have our work cut out for us." I lowered my voice to keep our conversation private. "Frankly, the more I think about this case, the more bizarre it seems. Here we are, a third of the way around the world, searching for some undefined 'shadow' stolen for *no* apparent reason from the Mexican President's own son! You really should have asked for more particulars before accepting that retainer." I was fully aware that this conversation was raking over old ground.

"The way it was offered," Geoff chuckled, "that would have proved a trifle difficult, don't you think?" He paused to lift a cordless shaver from his overnight bag. "Besides, cryptic messages do have their advantages. Our client may not have been free to express himself more clearly."

"You believe he's being spied upon?"

The razor buzzed in Weston's grasp as he attacked the bristles surrounding his goatee. In the subdued light he resembled a gangling, young Abe Lincoln dressed for a whistlestop jog.

"Surveillance is a possibility," he mused between strokes. "But then every public figure is rather much on display. And neither telegraph nor telephone operators are above passing on an occasional tidbit to reporters. The very vagueness of the communique convinces me of its importance. John, have another look at the thing, and you'll see what I mean."

Somewhat awkwardly he reached his free hand down the neck of his sweater and groped for the telegram. At length the yellow sheet emerged—firmly attached to a pen it had snagged from the pocket on the way up. While my partner returned the ballpoint to its proper place, I unfolded the paper, switched on my reading lamp, and started translating (my Spanish is poor to fair; my partner's fair to good):

"From Salvador Guerrero, D.F.
To Mr. Geoffrey Weston and John Taylor
Esq., Baker Street, London, England

AMIABLE GENTLEMEN MY SHADOW
HAS BEEN ABDUCTED STOP PLEASE

COME QUICKLY STOP FUNDS HAVE
BEEN DEPOSITED IN YOUR ACCOUNT
TO COVER EXPENSES"

I reread its contents, pondering the wording. (I happen
to be the "John Taylor" so addressed.)

"It does seem a mite brusque and ambiguous," I finally
conceded. "Decidedly un-Latin. . . . When you come right
down to it, we're not *really* employed at all. The man merely
wants to see our shining faces. But if he stuffed three
hundred thousand pesos in the bank to cover our airfares,
he's more than a little touched."

"Touched," Geoff concluded with a grin, "by everything
but his own shadow. And we're only two passersby asked to
come share young Peter Pan's grief. Notice that he purpose-
ly avoided addressing the telegram to Sleuths, Ltd. The
'Esquire' after your name was a nice flourish, too. A president's son arranges a meeting with an esquire. How positively diplomatic!"

I returned Weston's smile in spite of myself and assumed
a posture more in keeping with my station. Unfortunately a
decidedly Churchillian paunch under my vest curved the
ramrod a bit.

"At last," I returned good-naturedly, "you've come to
see a use for my title. And one with overtones of intrigue at
that!" I reached over and handed my pillow to a passing
stewardess. "But what's that about Salvador avoiding our
agency name? Perhaps he simply doesn't know it."

Geoff shook his head almost imperceptibly.

"That won't do, John. I would imagine that he and possibly his father must have examined our business from top
to bottom."

"You're sure?"

"How else would he know what bank we use? We don't
exactly shout that information to every client and street
bumpkin! Oh, the man's investigated us, all right. And the
money almost certainly came from the Mexican Embassy in
London. That involves the father since he's the only family
member with official connections. Mexican law is very strict
on that point."

I snapped my safety buckle closed and swallowed hard to

open my ears against the changing cabin pressure.

"This certainly puts matters in a new light," I reflected gravely. "It sounds as though we've been called in to investigate some national incident. But I'm still bothered about that balmy shadow. Guerrero's statement is so much nonsense! If the 'shadow' is some spy following him, our client should be relieved the blighter's disappeared. And if the shadow's a shadow, we're back to humoring a lunatic."

"With," Geoff beamed, "the father's doting approval. There are all kinds of interesting possibilities, aren't there?" He paused briefly to return the shaver to its leather case. "But I fancy neither of your theories will hold up. The President is unlikely to pay us a small fortune on a mad man's whim, even if he is a son. And, unfortunately, the term 'shadow' in Spanish can't refer to a chap specializing in surveillance. The only Castillian meaning that makes any sense at all is 'protection.' But again, one wonders how a man's protection can be stolen when he has the entire secret service at his disposal."

"Perhaps," I suggested, "there's a plot afoot to overthrow the government."

Weston considered for a moment, savoring the potential challenge.

"No," he decided at length, "that just doesn't ring true. Salvador stated distinctly that *his* shadow was abducted—not his father's, not the government's. Surely he wouldn't be so specific if he had in mind some general calamity. I'm inclined to suspect the kidnapping of some key person. But it remains to be seen how one such incident could threaten Guerreros' security."

"It remains," I reminded him pointedly, "because you've steadfastly refused to telephone the gentleman to find out. Surely you could have rung and at least asked a few cryptic questions of your own."

"Cryptic for cryptic," my partner replied, tongue-in-cheek. "And all for the sake of discovering the family plot. Are you sure the matter is that grave?"

I rolled my eyes and groaned in despair.

"Geoff, if Mexico has a law on the books against hit-and-run punning, you're a dead duck."

"Deadpan at times," Weston bantered, "but never a

dead duck. Ah, duck!" He smacked his lips. "Now there's a corpus delectable. Remind me to stop in for some pato while we're . . ."

"You're impossible! Forget the 'fowl' comments. Stop (it pains me to say it) 'ducking' the issue, and tell me why we're out here banging our heads together trying to figure out a riddle when we should already know the facts and be mapping out strategy for solving the crime!"

"Ah, why indeed!" My partner forced a seriousness into his tone, but the edges of his mouth continued to curve irrepressibly upward. "As nearly as I can figure, the Guerrero family wants us ignorant. Otherwise the father would have sent details by diplomatic courier. They probably don't trust our having the information before we're within range of their political power. Under those circumstances it seemed pointless to ring them up."

"Rather a suspicious lot," I concluded with a frown. "Yet we're obliging by flying right into their parlor."

Weston snapped his belt buckle closed somewhat belatedly. Turbulent air was beginning to buffet the Concorde, assaulting us with both the sound and sensation of being scraped across a washboard as we continued our descent.

"Most assuredly we're going," he replied decisively. "I admire pluck. And you have to admit it was plucky to give us a non-retainer. They would have lost their shirt to less scrupulous detectives. What's more, I'm curious about what's causing this mania for secrecy. It would be irritating to go through life wondering who the shadow was, now wouldn't it?"

"The Shadow," I informed him in my most resonant old-time-radio voice, "is Lamar Cranston. And he 'knows what evil lurks within the hearts of men.' That's more than we know about our employers."

"Of course it is," Geoff agreed. "But I've prayed concerning that telegram, and I have a sense of real peace about our venture." He looked at his watch, then remembered it was still on Greenwich time. "We'll know the kidnappee's identity soon enough. And a face-to-face chat with Salvador should fill in a few additional puzzle pieces as well."

I was about to respond but found myself cut short by a sinking sensation in the pit of my stomach. The airliner's delta wings must have cut through into an air pocket, for we dropped a good fifty feet straight down. Almost in reflex my hands shot to the arm rests and gripped them—hard. The engines continued their steady whine, though, and my internal butterflies fluttered to extinction as quickly as they had come. On the ground ahead of us blue-white strobe lights flashed in neat rows signaling our approach to the field. I breathed a prayer of my own, asking the Lord for firm air during those last crucial seconds of the glide.

* * * * *

The office was spacious and largely empty—except for cement posts holding up the ceiling and for sleepy passengers attempting to keep themselves upright. Forty fiberglass immigration desks stood in a row like supermarket checkout counters, but only three uniformed "clerks" were on hand to handle the flow. The aduanas were bored and perfunctory. Fortunately the lines moved swiftly. And our turn came before I had completely rehearsed honest, diplomatic answers that would protect Guerrero's secrecy. The spit-'n-polish official accepted our papers and glanced down with disinterest that quickly dissolved into amusement.

"Detectives—no me digan! You certainly don't look it." He smiled wryly at the private joke and scrawled something on a sheet hidden under the hooded desk front. By the time he looked up, his voice had nearly regained its practiced monotony. "Take your documents downstairs to customs and they'll be stamped with the place and date of entry. Have a nice stay in Mexico." Without waiting for a reply he made a notation on our papers, handed them to Weston, and looked through us at the next "customer."

I somewhat hesitantly followed Geoff's lead and pushed through the turnstile on my way to the stairs. We hadn't been asked a single question about our purpose for coming! That state of affairs, I was sure, wouldn't last. When our bags were opened, eyebrows would crank up to full mast and we'd be thoroughly interrogated as possible contrabandistas, illegally employed aliens. What tourists, after all, would be dragging around a portable crime laboratory! I was wrong, however. We breezed through customs and were soon clicking our heels across glistening marble floors toward the terminal's front entrance. Glass walls and aluminum gleamed on all sides and the building looked as though it would never end.

"Me thinks," I commented dryly, "that we weren't totally unexpected. You could have brought your Webley revolver and the inspector still wouldn't have batted an eyelash."

"You're probably right," Weston agreed. "One wonders where the welcoming committee is. They should have met us just outside the restricted area. Well, we can always follow the yellow brick signs to the cab stand."

"A wizard idea," I enthused, "provided that includes a trip to some hotel for what's left of the night."

We walked briskly past a row of curio shops and out the front door. And there we received two hearty welcomes. From across the street a twenty-foot-tall, dewy-lipped redhead enticed us to buy a Horno Acros oven. At her side Dina tractors posed for admiring glances. And so on down the line of at least thirty billboards. Somewhat closer at hand a large black limousine stood next to our curb in a place reserved for cabbies. When he saw us the chauffeur compared our faces with a photograph, got out of the motorcar and opened wide the side door in silent invitation. We obliged by entering.

"Where to?" Weston quipped in his best Spanish. "Now there's a line I've seldom used in the back seat."

Our driver slammed the door closed with just the correct amount of force. He had the high cheekbones and broad, flat nose of an Indian, but his expression and dress were formal and vaguely military.

"We," he informed us in broken English, "go to the—how ees eet said?—palacio. I ahm sorry ees no motorcycle escort, but they tol me to come alone." (Since he wanted to try out his English, we decided to humor him. We'd be trying out our Spanish later.)

I sniffed in mild annoyance at the chemical odor hovering outside the airport.

"That's perfectly understandable. Let's start immediately before we all end up smelling like a new plastic raincoat."

"But, of course. ¡Cómo no!"

He seemed puzzled by my "coat" reference, but was only

too ready to stash our luggage in the rear, slide quickly behind the steering wheel, and gun the engine. We bolted away from the curb and drove a full block the wrong way before making a U-turn and passing back under the billboards. The road quickly turned into a four-lane, one-way affair that gave me the feeling we were driving across a soccer field. To the left a parking garage pancaked high into the air. Road signs reassured us that Airport Boulevard lay straight ahead.

"How is it," Weston ventured thoughtfully, "that we're not going to San Pedro de los Pinos. I was under the impression that the President and his family lived there."

Our driver looked both ways at the intersection, accelerated through a red light, and sped past a parked DC-3 airplane that someone had converted into a restaurant.

"They do, Meester. But the son ees vice president of the Mexican Bank—which ees very near the palacio. Eet ees better to stay at the palacio, no, and walk to work?"

"It is," I commented archly, "if everyone here drives like you do. In the future, would you mind stopping at stoplights?"

He eyed me in the rearview mirror with surprise.

"But why, Señor, if there ees no policeman?"

"Because it's the law!"

The driver pondered that a moment.

"Sí. Eet ees la ley. But which ees more smart, a machine or a persona? And the light, she no has eyes to see a carro like I do."

I groaned softly. "Just as a favor to us."

"Oh, that ees different!" He raised both hands over his head for emphasis. "As a favor I weel even be your, how you say, tourista guide."

"That will," Geoff quickly assured him, "be just fine, so long as you keep one hand on the wheel."

"You two," our black-haired driver chuckled, "are a leetle nervous for detectives. Do not worry; I never have accidente." He pointed out the window in the darkness. "Over there behind those trees ees the palacio deportive— the sports center. Eet looks like a giant copper pine . . . apple. During the Olympeec games. . . ."

We had just taken an exit ramp onto Fray Servando—an

immense twelve-lane motorway with triple islands and scores of bushy palm trees. Non-descript shops lined the sidewalks. And every store sported its own corrugated-steel garage door dutifully rolled down over what must have been display windows. Mexicans, it appeared, were security conscious. They had reason to be, for opulence and poverty intermixed like grains of rice and salt in a shaker. Block after block the same stores repeated themselves with monotonous regularity. Shoe emporiums, clothiers, and book shoppes vied with fruit stands and restaurants for dominance.

". . . And that domed building over there," our guide continued, "ees one of the deestreect headquarters de policía. Eet ees very beautiful, no?"

As we approached the center of town, the buildings began to grow to six or seven stories. And I could make out the lighted windows of a few skyscrapers on the horizon. Then the road started to descend into a tunnel. Our driver turned quickly just short of the entrance and we doglegged up a ramp onto 20th of November Avenue. Within minutes a street-wide slice of cathedral became visible several blocks ahead. Since I knew the palace was kitty-corner to a large church, I suspected we were nearing our destination. We were.

The national palace soon loomed before us, bathed in the rays of a hundred floodlights. Drab lava rock rose to a height of perhaps fifty feet punctuated by rows of windows, scattered gun ports, and a block-long array of scarlet awnings. Here was a new-world Kremlin in its Sunday best! Two soldiers with automatic rifles stood guard at each of three massive metal-studded doors. We drove to the one nearest the church and pulled up onto the sidewalk for inspection.

I had the eerie feeling of being a Connecticut Yankee in King Arthur's court. The elements of what I saw just didn't mix well. Not thirty feet away a stairway dug through the sidewalk and descended into the city's modern tube system. Yet in front of me a seventeenth-century fortress with bars on the lower windows squatted immovable and (if such a thing is possible) ornately austere. Centuries-old sentry posts straddled the entrance, but were now mere base relief decorations in stone walls. The guards stood in front of them, open to gunfire from anywhere across the square. And

those guards! They were an enigma too. One was regular army. The other, judging from his white helmet emblazoned with the letters PM, belonged to the military police.

The MP had by now broken away from his partner and come to pay us a visit. Without saying a word he shined his flashlight in our window and peered gloomily about. Still scowling, he turned to the driver and spoke in clipped tones.

"Quiénes son, Andrés?" (Who are they, Andrew?)

The chauffeur's reply was just as curt.

"Los invitados." (The invited ones.)

The sergeant checked our luggage compartment and then waved us on. At the gesture, his partner opened wide the double doors and we drove slowly through into a spacious courtyard.

The motorcar parked in front of a bronze statue of some seated hero, and we clambered out before the driver could do the customary honors. Weston looked critically about him.

"This place, John, could do with a little more light. A few iron lanterns dangling over doorways simply don't do the job." He craned his neck upward and turned around in a circle. "Look, the top balcony doesn't even have those! An enterprising sniper could pick us off like flies on a picnic table and we wouldn't even see him."

"Provided," I pointed out, "the man could get in to begin with. And that wouldn't be easy."

Andrew opened the boot and began hauling out baggage.

"Eet has never happen," he volunteered. "Eef you follow me, I take you to the oficina of Señor Guerrero."

"But surely," I protested, "he won't be there at this time of night."

"Eef not, I get heem for you."

So saying, Andrew loaded up with suitcases and began walking toward one of the archways behind the statue. I grabbed a valise and we followed through the tunnel. Beyond lay another almost identical courtyard circumscribed by iron-banistered balconies aloft and barred windows on the ground floor. We passed through two additional courtyards, then stepped into a passageway that jogged to the left. Andrew stopped in front of a door marked simply 1401 and knocked respectfully. Almost at once I heard movement inside. A dark silhouette glided across the translucent panel in the door, and someone worked the latch. The panel slid inward to reveal a young man who turned out to be our client.

"Ah, it is you! Come in, my friends. As we say, 'It is your house.' " Salvador hugged us in turn—slapping Geoff and me heartily on the back. "It was good of you to be so prompt. Andrés, would you please take our visitors' bags up to room 612. They'll be staying awhile." Salvador's English was flawless.

As I handed the chauffeur my valise, the President's son retreated across velvet carpet to take a seat behind his desk. Although a slender fellow in his mid-twenties, he was imposing—and dressed like a fashion plate. His form-fitted suit, flaired trousers, and styled black hair marked him as a devotee of the disco look. The hint of pride, aquiline nose and firm jaw had another source. I'd seen variations of that face stamped on a thousand coins. When the door clicked closed behind us, Salvador lost a good bit of his joviality.

"Have a seat, gentlemen." He gestured toward two straight-backed chairs, making an attempt at Latin hospitality. "I regret I can't offer you any coffee, but the milk's not hot yet. How was your trip?"

"It was," Weston smiled as he eased onto the cushion, "like diving into a well and starting to wonder halfway down if there was water at the bottom. John and I spent the time speculating about your shadow. You really should have written in English. It would have narrowed down the possibilities a mite."

"And," Guerrero added soberly, "have reduced the sense of mystery." He folded his hands and leaned forward. "To be truthful, gentlemen, I wanted to use every psychological trick I could to insure you'd come. Mr. Weston, your name's not a household word around here, but as a banker I make it a point to read the *Wall Street Journal.* I was fascinated by their article on how you recovered the missing island of Scorpus."

"And," I sighed, "you jolly well figured that chaps who could find a mile-long island would have no trouble with a six-foot shadow."

"Something like that." Our client's gaze met mine without faltering. "At least that was my hope. But I've kept you in suspense long enough." He paused briefly to squeeze the bridge of his nose between thumb and forefinger. "Excuse me. I've had a slight headache this evening. As I was about to say, the problem isn't nearly so bizarre as I've perhaps led you to believe. I'm a man who values friendship very highly. And someone who's almost a brother to me has been kidnapped. I want you to find him. It's as simple as that."

Geoff stroked his goatee and considered Salvador's statement.

"And what," he mused, "of the reference to a shadow or to protection?"

"Oh, that. Memo Hernandez, the victim, was my bodyguard."

"I see." Weston eyed our host sharply. "And you had no other reason than friendship for calling us in?"

"None." The President's son smiled with a candor that seemed genuine. "I'm sorry if you're disappointed. Simple regard for others does appear rather out of place today, doesn't it?"

"Not at all," I disagreed. "Christ went one step further and laid down His life for His *enemies*. I'd say your attitude was rather noble."

"If," Geoff broke in, "that's your attitude. I happen to believe you're lying." Salvador and I both turned toward him in amazement. Then our client's dimples evaporated and his face turned expressionless.

"I beg your pardon."

"You should," Weston informed him. "I don't fancy traveling all this distance to be dallied with. The local police are fully competent to handle the case you've just described and, unless you tell us the rest of the story, they shall be the ones who do the investigating."

"But surely, now that you're here . . ."

Geoff stood up.

"Guerrero, I won't be manipulated. Either you tell us what prompted your extraordinary secrecy and our breeze through customs, or we return home on the next flight."

Salvador picked up a letter opener with his right hand and began rapping it nervously on the desk. He seemed torn between letting us go and divulging more.

"All right," he concluded at last. "Sit down and I'll 'fill you in'—as the Americans say. I should have realized any detective worth hiring wouldn't be easily fooled."

"We can assure you," I added as Weston regained his chair, "that whatever we hear will remain in the strictest confidence. As foreigners we certainly have no political axe to grind."

"That's true, at least," our host reflected. "But it would be a shame if Memo held up during questioning and the kidnappers later extracted the information they want from one of you."

Weston pulled a bag of peanuts from his pocket and tore open the cellophane with an air of unconcern.

"You may keep your comments general enough to preclude that," he drawled. "But do be honest; if clients are deceitful I double my fee."

"Yes, I believe you do." Salvador studied my partner with the shrewd eye of a businessman. "Mr. Weston, my bodyguard some time ago came into possession of certain state secrets—secrets that if made public would be highly embarrassing to the government. I can't reveal their nature, but I assure you your efforts could prevent the toppling of my father's presidency."

"In that case," Geoff beamed, "let's get started immediately. How long has Memo been missing?"

"Since the evening before last. He drove out of here at the end of his shift and that's the last anyone has seen of him."

"And his motorcar?"

"It was discovered abandoned in the colonia Churubusco—not two blocks from his house."

"I take it," Weston prompted, "no one saw who parked it."

"No one. And the police were unable to find any evidence in the car itself."

"There has been, of course, no ransom note."

"None."

Geoff rose purposefully to his feet and leaned over the mahogany desk to shake the young man's hand.

"You can be assured," he promised, "that we'll do our best to rescue your friend. If he's alive, I think we'll find him. But we will require some additional assistance from you."

Guerrero's grip was firm.

"Anything within reason, Señor." A smile flickered again into his eyes. "I appreciate the help."

"John and I," Weston continued levelly, "will be sleeping in until dawn. Between now and then I would like you to obtain certain items for us. We require a map of the city, a motorcar, the victim's address, the address at which his vehicle was abandoned, the location of the police garage in which it now resides, the names of Memo's closest relatives and friends, and a letter of introduction to the inspector heading up the investigation. Please slide the information under our door. The motorcar may remain in the courtyard."

"That's just as well," Salvador grinned. "It would never fit in the elevator. Have a nice rest. It's good to have you on the team. Andrés will show you to your rooms."

Chapter 2

The Bop, the Boot, and the Drop

I rolled over in bed, opened my eyes a crack, and reached out to punch off the alarm. The last jangle died a merciful death in mid-ring—to be replaced gradually, as consciousness surfaced, by screeches and motor rumble on the street below. Whether or not I liked it, it was morning. Time to get up!

Under the covers I struggled into my trousers and shoes—loathe to step barefoot onto icy tiles. A palace! This was the *chilliest* lap of luxury I'd ever endured. Heating ducts were nonexistent, and the single space heater in the corner wasn't working. The entire room, in fact, gave itself to a rather seedy elegance. The ornate furniture contrasted incongruously with the yellow paint on the walls which was beginning to powder; and the recessed light panels overhead were better suited to an office than to an apartment.

Finally decent, I stepped over to the window and pushed aside the curtains to let in the warming sunlight. I had my first glimpse of Mexico City by day and quickly forgot the inconveniences of the moment. The entire square out front was surfaced with concrete—not in itself a very pretty sight. But a flagpole rising from its center held aloft the most impressive banner I'd ever seen. A full forty feet long and nearly as wide, it undulated proudly in the breeze. And with every flutter its fierce nylon eagle seemed to tighten his grip on a snake that tried to wriggle free. The snake never succeeded, but then neither did the bird enjoy his lunch. The emblem struck me as an unintended commentary on the state. Politicians might urge the country "upward and forward" to a prosperity hovering at beak's tip, but in my view corruption and poor management invariably prevented the tasting.

"Lord," I breathed, "it would take only a few Christians in the government to make such a great difference in the future of this country. Please use us while we're here to plant some seeds."

I scanned the panorama before me. The ornate, multi-towered cathedral to the right had an angel, saint, or spire perched on every ledge; but it was a dead, drab gray. Government offices to the left and rear of the square echoed the dreary shade. And even the beautiful Latin American Tower, peeking over the skyline from a mile away, seemed hazy and indistinct. The very air matched the tint of the buildings as bumper-to-bumper traffic clogged streets and belched fumes. This city needs some color, I decided! And not merely outwardly, but "color" and purpose for living like I had found when I surrendered to Christ.

My thoughts were interrupted as Geoff strode briskly through the doorway from the shared living room.

"Good to see you're up, John! We have a busy morning ahead of us." He pulled a map from his coat pocket and tossed it to me. "Here's one of the items our client dropped off. Judging from the locations marked and from that street out there, we'll be using public transportation."

"My," I remarked with an approving glance in his direction, "a sport coat and tie! To what do we owe the sartorial splendor?"

"I do not wish," Geoff winked, "to be mistaken for an American tourist. Now about that map—you'll notice the police station and garage are only one tube stop south of us. We come out right on their doorstep. So I'd suggest we make the acquaintance of a certain Inspector Porfirio Robledo before going off on our own."

"That," I concluded, "sounds reasonable enough. I take it this Mr. Robledo is heading up the locals' investigation."

"Indeed," Weston agreed. "He's just the man to get us into the parking garage. I want a look at Memo's motorcar."

I slid my arms into a shirt and started buttoning down and tucking in. "After two days of being dismantled by police, I doubt there'll be much left of it for us."

"You may be right," Geoff admitted, "but we've got to

start somewhere. And I don't fancy spending the day inter-
viewing Hernandez' relatives. Salvador left me a list a yard
long! While you finish dressing I'll grab the fingerprint kit
and a few other essentials out of the valise. I don't imagine
taking luggage along goes over well in the underground transit." He turned and walked off toward his bedroom before I
thought to ask about breakfast.

* * * * *

The land of the troglodytes, it turned out, was both
cleaner smelling and more colorful than its above-ground
counterpart. Entire ceilings glowed. We walked on brilliant-
ly polished, chocolate ripple marble. Historical murals,
escalators and pyramid-filled showcases were set off by blue
and burnt-orange trim. One thing was the same, however:
crowds were enormous. As Geoff and I slid tickets into the
turnstiles, we were pushed on through by the others behind
us like lemmings on the way to the sea. When we reached
the platform a flight of stairs farther down, the current reversed. We'd hardly arrived before a sleek orange train glided to a stop and doors opened spewing forth well-dressed
men and women hurrying somewhere. The two of us managed to jostle our way through and squeeze into the coach
just as a buzzer sounded and doors shut, enclosing us like
stalks of asparagus in a tin can.

"This," I commented to Weston, "is ridiculous. I can't
even see the seats. And my pockets have probably already
been picked three times."

Geoff tightened his grip on the rail overhead as we
lurched forward. "Look on the bright side, old bean. The
ride's smooth. And any would-be pickpockets on board
probably don't have room to lower their hands. Notice there
isn't even any graffiti on the walls."

"I'll comfort you with that information if it's your wallet
that turns up missing," I rejoined.

The train seemed hardly to have reached top speed before it started slowing. In perhaps thirty seconds we slid to a
stop at Pino Suárez station and my partner and I made our
escape. Soon we were back on the street walking toward a
new, seven-story building whose only claim to style consist-
ed of pebblestone cement strips between the rows of windows. Due to the vagaries of real estate, an ancient stone

chapel stood rooted on the sidewalk directly in front of it. We passed the church and strode purposefully through the front door of the police headquarters. By that time my eyes were smarting from the smog.

As we stepped inside we almost collided with two hulking men in blue. That might not have been too bad except that they were carrying sub-machine guns. I was only too ready to be cooperative. I hoped my partner felt the same way.

The meaner looking of the two leveled his weapon at us. "¿Cuál es su negocio? This area is restricted."

Weston started to reach his hand in his coat for the letter of introduction but thought better of it.

"We're here to see Inspector Robledo," he stated levelly in Spanish. "If you search my pocket, you'll find the authorization."

"We'll do more than that, Señor," his partner jeered in Spanish. "Lean against the wall and spread your legs. Jaime, I'll keep them in my sights while you check for weapons."

Jaime proceeded to pat us thoroughly, but all he came up with was a New Testament and a pocket knife. He seemed to be extremely interested, however, in the knife—opening it and testing for sharpness with his thumb.

"This," he frowned, "is very bad, my friend. You thought perhaps to give it to one of the prisoners?"

"If we've blundered into the gaol, I'm sorry," Geoff replied coolly, "but that could have been prevented by a few signs. Now will you please direct us to the Inspector?"

The partner now approached us with his sub-machine gun lowered only slightly. His heavy eyelids partially covered an expressionless stare. "Perhaps it is only a mistake. But you have broken the law by bringing a weapon in here. We will have to detain you, unless, of course . . ."

"I understand." Weston dipped his hand in his coat pocket. "There's the matter of a fine. I think this should prove sufficient."

He pulled out Guerrero's letter and handed it to Jaime, who started to refuse but then noticed the presidential letterhead. The message was quickly unfolded and scanned. Jaime gestured to his partner to put aside his artillery.

"These men appear to be legitimate, Juan." He returned the letter to Geoff and made an effort to smile. "I'm sorry we have inconvenienced you, Mr. Weston. The knife will, however, have to remain with us while you're in the building. Those are the regulations. You may pick it up as you leave."

"Of course," Geoff added. "But we'll still need to know the room number of Inspector Robledo."

"He's in 317." The guard pointed with his thumb to the wall behind him. "Take the elevator to the third floor and turn right. Have a nice visit."

"Thank you very much."

We left the policemen behind and walked rapidly to the lift. When we were safely inside and the door had glided closed, I felt a wave of relief.

"Now," I commented, "the proximity of that church makes sense. Everyone must stop to pray before they come in here. If they don't, they should."

Geoff chuckled. "The chaps were a bit heavy-handed, weren't they? But then we might really have been hooligans."

"In which case they never should have asked for money."

"True," my partner conceded. "But when some of their bosses are living like millionaries from their graft, what can you expect?"

The lift slowed to a stop. We stepped out and began strolling down a narrow hallway lined with neatly lettered glass doors.

"That's it over there," I pointed. "The Criminal Investigation Division. Let's hope it's criminals that are investigated and not the investigation that's criminal."

"I assume," Weston smiled, "it's the former. Try not to let our single incident sour you."

We walked boldly through the doorway and up to an L-shaped counter that stood between us and the detectives' desks.

"Señorita," I addressed a clerk who wasn't busy, "we're detectives from Great Britain here to see Inspector Robledo."

"But, of course," she brightened. "He's in his office. I'm sure he'd be delighted to visit with you. If you wait a moment, I'll go ask."

"That," Geoff assured her, "will be just fine. To save time, you might also deliver this letter."

She smiled and took it from his outstretched hand.

"There's a pot of coffee on the table behind you. If I'm not right back, you're welcome to sit down and have a cup."

"Thank you," I responded with feeling. "*You're* very gracious." My slave-driver of a partner totally missed the oblique reference to our lack of breakfast.

The young lady patted her short hair-do into place and hurried across the room toward a frosted-glass cubicle in the corner. She disappeared inside only to emerge a few seconds later and wave good-bye to us.

"That," I complained in English, "is the last straw! We won't even be able to see the bloke!"

Weston, however, grabbed my arm and began steering me through the counter's swinging door.

"Don't be absurd, John," he whispered. "You just haven't spent enough time in Latin America. She's motioning us to come."

"With a wave?"

"The fingers," Geoff sighed, "are beckoning toward her. So what if the hand's turned down. Remember, we're in another culture."

"As if I could ever forget," I muttered.

We nodded our thanks to the clerk as we passed and sauntered into a small office lined with filing cabinets. The single desk in the middle was piled high with assorted clutter ranging from paper cups and candy wrappers to wanted posters and report forms. Not a particularly tidy chap myself, I felt an instant affinity for the place. Behind the desk a thin gentleman with receding hairline was finishing Salvador's note. At home he would have been just barely tall enough to make the force. His temples were graying and he seemed slightly haggard. As we approached, he looked up at us over the gold rims of his spectacles.

"Así que ustedes son los dos héroes legendarios—so you are the two legendary heroes." His Spanish was cultured and melodic. "I've been wanting to meet you for a long time to see if flesh and blood lives up to the folk tales." He rose to his feet and grasped Geoff's hand between both of his. "It's so good of you to come!"

"It's good to be here," my partner replied warmly. "And the answer's 'no.' Anything you've heard has been greatly exaggerated."

"Oh, Señor, and modesty wasn't even mentioned by the newspapers!"

"That," I commented dryly, "is because Geoff succumbs to it so infrequently." I extended my arm for a repeat of the greeting. "We would very much like to work with you on this Hernandez case."

"So I've read in Señor Salvador's letter." The Inspector released my hand and sat down. "While we talk, perhaps you'd care for some sweet bread and coffee." Without waiting for an answer, he flipped on the intercom. "Lupe, would you bring some refreshments for our guests, por favor?"

"That," I smiled, "is the best news I've had all morning. If your briefing on the investigation is half as encouraging, we'll have the crime solved by noon."

"Providing," Profirio amended, "there has been a crime."

Weston and I pulled up seats and settled down in front of the overflowing desk.

"I must admit," Geoff acknowledged, "that thought has crossed my mind."

"What thought?" I demanded. "What in the world are you two babbling about? Of course there's been a crime! That's why we're here."

In answer the Inspector rummaged through a pile of papers and pulled out a thick folder. His voice was matter-of-fact.

"In here you will find over one hundred twenty pages of testimony from everyone even remotely connected with Memo or the 'kidnapping.' And what does it tell us?" He poked the folder with his finger for emphasis. "Guillermo had tremendous ambition, but he was strictly 'from Monterrey.' Excuse me—that is to say, he was stingy. Nights of overtime never resulted in so much as an extra centavo toward supporting his family."

"Then," I concluded, "he was married."

"No. Not at all. He lived at home with his parents."

The door behind us opened and the pretty brunette clerk entered carrying a tray of goodies with a fresh-baked aroma that followed behind her.

"I haven't added any sugar to the coffee," she volunteered. "But there are cubes in the bowl. Is that all, Inspector, or is there something else you would like?"

"No. That's just fine, gracias."

The young lady set the tray down on the edge of the desk and retreated to the other room. As she did, I picked up a pastry and gave silent thanks.

"Now, where was I?" Robledo considered as he stirred his coffee. "Oh yes—it's the custom here for a son to give his entire pay envelope to his parents and then receive an allowance. We have discovered that Memo, however, kept back a substantial portion."

"In other words," Weston prompted, "Hernandez may well have had enough money set aside to finance his own disappearance."

"Absolutely."

"But what possible motive," I inquired between bites, "could he have for doing that? If, as you say, he was ambitious, he would be most unlikely to leave a lucrative job. And if he did, why wouldn't he simply quit and move out of town?"

"That," Porfirio answered, "is something I'm not prepared to answer at the moment. But I find it interesting that only last week he bragged to his sister he was about to become wealthy. Perhaps you have been able to learn something at the palace as to why they are so committed to 'rescuing' him?"

"Perhaps," Geoff repeated noncommittally. "So you suspect the man of either blackmail or treason."

Thoughtfully, Robledo took a sip of coffee and set the cup down.

"Those are awfully harsh words, Mr. Weston. Officially, I don't suspect anything. But if I possessed some secret information and intended to convert it to cash, I'd probably disappear first under suspicious circumstances. That way the 'kidnapper' would shoulder the blame for my actions."

My partner gestured toward the folder.

"What other findings in that report should we know about?"

"There are not all that many," Porfirio admitted with an

eloquent Latin-American shrug. "The abandoned automobile did not contain any fingerprints—not even those of the owner. We found no bloodstains. And there was virtually no evidence of a struggle."

"In other words," Weston coaxed, "you found what a professional kidnapper would have left behind and not what an amateur might be expected to stage."

The Inspector selected a cookie from the tray and bit into it.

"You know, you're right. No había pensado eso. If Memo wasn't kidnapped, he's much craftier than I've imagined."

"That brings us to the question," I noted, "of where the investigation is going from here."

"Probably nowhere," our host replied with candor. "We've shown Memo's picture to half the city, and no one remembers seeing him. What's more, we've nearly finished questioning everyone who lives along his route home from work. If someone forced his way into the young man's automobile, he did it without being seen."

Geoff finished off the last of his coffee.

"It appears then," he reflected, "that the motorcar is the only concrete evidence at this time. Would it be possible for John and me to have a look at it?"

"¿Cómo no? Of course!" The Inspector got to his feet and eased a jacket off the back of his chair. "We can go right now if you wish. I'd enjoy the walk." He glanced balefully at the paperwork on the desk. "Fresh air will do us all good."

"That," Weston assured him, "will be just fine."

"Provided," I amended as I reached for another sweet bread, "we munch as we go. These pastries are simply delicious."

The three of us left the office together, marched down several cross corridors, and descended two flights of stairs. We came out at last on the opposite side of the building—directly across from the garage. Porfirio then stepped boldly into the street like a crossing guard and directed traffic with emphatic gestures until Geoff and I had reached the other side. He quickly rejoined us and we continued on our stroll toward the entrance gate. It was just that—a gate set in an eight-foot cement wall surrounding two or three acres of asphalt. As we approached, we passed what resembled an

old train station ticket window set into the wall. According
to Robledo, the tickets issued there were of the tin vari-
ety—as errant drivers paid fines in exchange for the plates
to their impounded vehicles. A few steps farther along we
passed through the gateway and waved good-naturedly to
the policeman standing guard. The Inspector, however,
didn't so much as slow down to ask directions. He seemed to
know exactly where he was going, and we tagged along,
weaving in and out between rows of motorcars.

"It must be quite a job," I noted admiringly between
breaths, "for you to keep track of where everything is in
here—particularly since there aren't any license numbers!"

Porfirio squeezed between a battered Ford and a sleek
new Malibu and turned right.

"Oh, it's really not that difficult," he remarked as a gust
of wind tussled his hair. "If a car is evidence in a case, we
keep it in that section up ahead and record its exact location. If we bring a vehicle in for any other reason, we just
park it and the owner searches. That gives drivers an extra
incentive for not double parking."

"I would say so!" I shook my head. "How can you be sure
some chap doesn't drive off with the wrong motorcar?"

"That's easy. By law registration cards are kept in the
glove compartment. So we check them against the person's
driving permit. Things really get interesting, though, if the
fellow is missing half his permit."

"*Half* his permit? How on earth could that happen?"

"Generally because someone is short of money. If he
can't pay an infraction, the traffic patrolman takes one of
the cards to his driver's license as collateral."

"I assume then," Weston interrupted sagely, "that a
bloke who comes here with a single card is in for a triple
fine."

"Absolutely," Porfirio concurred. The corners of his
mouth twitched with amusement. "We include driving
without a license in the list. What's more, he's got to dig his
permit out of a three-foot pile. Ah, that's Hernandez' car up
there—the Plymouth with the rust on the side. If you don't
mind, I'll stand outside and watch. I hate it myself when
someone looks over my shoulder, but I'd really like to study
your methods."

"We'd welcome it," Geoff assured him. "As a matter-of-fact, we may need your advice from time to time so we don't simply repeat what has already been done. Have you got the keys?"

"Yes, of course. They're right here." The Inspector extracted a chain from his pocket and delivered it over in mid-stride. "The round one is for the trunk."

"Then," Weston concluded, "let's use that one. I want a look at the boot first anyway." When we arrived at the battered sedan, he twisted open the lock and gingerly raised the luggage compartment lid. The interior was dusty in the extreme—and nearly empty.

"Have you," Geoff asked Robledo without taking his eyes off the sight, "tested the spare tire for fingerprints?"

Porfirio peered in as if trying to jog his memory.

"No. I don't believe so. We were mainly interested in finding blood back—"

"Good," Weston acknowledged. "Then you haven't moved the tire. Neither shall I. It hasn't been used in months."

While we looked on, he pulled his magnifier from his pocket and began inspecting the floor immediately in front of the spare. He peered long and intently—scanning from front to back like some nearsighted diner trying to read a Japanese menu.

"This is most interesting," he muttered at last. "John, take a peek at the center area and tell me what you think."

I accepted his lens and bent over without really knowing what to expect. However, it didn't take long to find out.

"Either dust is starting to develop now in plaid patterns," I marvelled, "or those crisscross lines indicate the recent presence of some fabric."

"Not only that," my partner added with a wrinkled brow, "but cloth pressed into the dust with considerable force. Notice how deep and well-defined the ridges are. It's quite possible someone dead or unconscious has taken a recent ride back here and left us a clothing print. Inspector, you might photograph the weave and compare it with what's left of Memo's wardrobe. If he bought his shirts and trousers in pairs, I think you'll find a match."

"¡Sin duda!" Porfirio's voice behind us betrayed excitement. "It will be done immediately. Would you lend me your magnifying glass a moment? I would like a look of my own."

"Certainly," Geoff agreed good-naturedly and handed it over his shoulder. "While you're doing that, we'll toddle up front. John, I'll inspect under the bonnet." He tossed me the keys and a spare glass. "Be a good chap and see to the passenger area. Oh, and if there's a bonnet latch, you might give it a yank."

We left the Inspector briefly and went to work. There *was* a latch and I pulled it. Geoff was soon sprawled over the motor like some filling-station Cassius probing the mechanism with "a lean and hungry look." For my part, I was content to study the dirt on the carpeting inch by careful inch. Every now and then I'd pick up a piece with pinchers and place it in an evidence envelope. There didn't seem to be anything exciting, however. Next, I checked the ashtrays. They contained virtually nothing.

"We've emptied them out for testing," Robledo volunteered from outside the window. His nose was so close to the pane that his glasses were fogging from breath backlash. "We've also checked under the seats and dash, dusted every metal or glass surface for prints, and vacuumed the cushions for hair and lint."

"That," I remarked cheerfully, "would seem to leave me with the tip of the cigarette lighter and the roof. How much did you find in the trays?"

"Nothing in the rear. The one in the dash was about half full."

"By nothing, what do you mean?" Weston inserted while coming around to the driver's door. "Had they been merely dumped out or scrubbed with detergent?"

"Polished," Robledo declared, "to a mirror shine."

"Then," Geoff considered while wiping grease from his hands, "I certainly do want a glance at the lighter. Better yet, John, you get the scrapings. I'll slide into the back seat and admire that roof the Inspector has so graciously left us. Porfirio, might I bother you for return of the lens? Thank you."

There were, it turned out, a few whitened particles still clinging to the end of the lighter. I tried my best to avoid those imbedded deep between the coils and to select only the most recent specimens. Meanwhile Geoff was gazing upward with an intensity that couldn't have been greater had he been Michaelangelo painting the Sistine Chapel. Every square centimeter came in for close scrutiny. I finished bagging the ash and sat twiddling my thumbs as he searched on, oblivious to all else. Finally the Inspector could stand it no longer.

"Mr. Weston." He stuck his hand in through the doorway. "Are you going to continue all day? It's just an ordinary ceiling."

Geoff jumped at the sound, then sheepishly slid his magnifier back into his pocket.

"I'm sorry, old chap, for ignoring you. Actually, I could have stopped moments ago, but I wanted to be sure."

"Sure of what?" I asked. "All I see is dirty plastic."

"Except," my partner corrected, "for one short, dust-free strip where the fabric has recently been scuffed." He pointed to a spot behind and slightly to the right of the driver's seat. "Notice the slant back and away from the door, as though someone has poked it with a shovel handle while loading up. Yet the scar is more pronounced toward the rear, which shouldn't happen if first impact occurred in the front. What's more, surface abrasions lean forward."

"Very interesting," Porfirio observed in a tone bordering on boredom. "So someone scraped the roof while *removing* the shovel. Unless you're implying the person has buried Memo, I don't see what significance—"

"Precisely," Weston broke in. "You don't see. A shovel tip PULLED across the roof wouldn't scuff, because movement would follow the handle's grain rather than cutting across it. What we have here is far more significant, and it pretty well proves what happened the day of the kidnapping."

Robledo studied Geoff for a few seconds as though trying to decide whether to take him seriously. Then his lips broke into a smile.

"You know, you amaze me, Mr. Weston. You can get more mileage from a single clue than any man I've ever met. Who is the kidnapper? Some one-armed terrorist with a stocking over his head?"

Geoff ignored the irony.

"That," he remarked levelly, "is highly unlikely. A mask isn't called for. I would guess that there were two kidnappers—one right-handed. They must have been known and trusted by the victim. And the right-handed one smoked. Aside from that I can deduce nothing. You'll have to count arms when you catch the chaps."

Porfirio blinked, then looked my way to see if I were a party to the joke.

"And can you," he continued uneasily, "say just how these 'two kidnappers' carried out their plot?"

"Only in general terms," Weston admitted with an almost imperceptible twinkle in his eye. "Memo most likely picked them up from the side of the road. When the motorcar paused for a stoplight, they bopped him over the head and then drove to the nearest alley to transfer his body to the boot. That accomplished, they took him somewhere in the city and subsequently discarded the Plymouth."

"Are you stringing me along?" the Inspector demanded. "No one could deduce all that from a scratch on the roof."

"Robledo has a point," I agreed. "I can see why you suspect a smoker. Polished ashtrays in a coach this old are hardly normal. But as to the rest—"

"As to the rest," Geoff declared in his best professional manner, "that scuff was made by a rock or some other rough object as a bloke in the back seat used it to dent Hernandez' skull. And since there are neither witnesses to foul play nor marks on this motorcar to show it was forced off the road, the passenger was quite possibly an invited guest. You've already surmised he was a smoker. From the angle of the scrape, he had to be right-handed. He acted while the sedan was stopped or there would have been an accident. He and his accomplice then found a secluded spot and moved their captive to the boot. The evidence back there demands as much."

The Inspector paused to digest the rapid-fire lecture.

"I can appreciate the logic," he nodded finally, "provided the scrape is what you think it is. We'll check it for microscopic particles. But I fail to see the need for an accomplice or to understand why you feel Memo is still in the city."

"Oh, that!" Weston waved his hand in dismissal. "There

may not have been two kidnappers, but if someone else was in the motorcar, it's easier to understand why Hernandez' attacker was positioned where he was. The front seat was already occupied! As to Memo's whereabouts, I never said he was still in the city. He could be in Newcastle by now for all I know. But this rattletrap," he gestured around him, "burns more than petrol. The engine looks as well lubricated on the outside as within. Yet the dipstick reads full. Men about to dump a vehicle are unlikely to add oil, so I conclude they probably didn't drive their victim far in it. Just how far I can't say, but a road test might provide some hints."

Robledo forgot himself and slapped down hard on the roof.

"¡Caramba! Now I believe everything I've heard about you. Together we shall solve this case. I know it! And someday we can tell our grandchildren stories of this our highest adventure!"

Geoff extricated himself from the motorcar and patted the Inspector good-naturedly on the back.

"Compadre, I'm looking forward to working with you. You're a real gentleman. But if I ever have grandchildren, they'll hear that this experience was only second best."

"Oh, and what was the first?"

"Look up the report," Weston invited. "It will hardly seem like paperwork."

Porfirio appeared mystified as he ran a comb through his hair trying to "lower" his forehead.

"But where, Señor? I have only the records for Mexico City. Surely this is your first case here."

"It is," my partner acknowledged. "But you shouldn't have any difficulty finding the information. It's in chapter five of Paul's second letter to the Corinthians."

"I see." A smile slowly crept across the Inspector's face. "*Now* you're making a joke, no? You're talking about religion."

"Investigate and find out," Weston challenged. "Then we can discuss your findings. But right now John and I have an appointment to clean the cracks in a sidewalk. By the way, some policemen in the gaol lobby have a certain pocket knife. We won't be returning that way, so if you could retrieve it for us I'd be most obliged."

"Sí, por cierto," Robledo agreed. "You are a complicated person, Mr. Weston, but by the time we meet again, perhaps I shall know you better."

"Until then," Geoff responded, "happy hunting."

Since I had by now rejoined the two outside the vehicle, we exchanged farewell handshakes all around after the Inspector had kindly pointed out on our map where we were to go. Geoff and I then headed for the gate while Porfirio paused to relock the Plymouth. His next move, I knew, would be to summon the lab boys to make additional tests. Ours would involve searching the area where the motorcar had been abandoned. Just before we left the garage, I turned impulsively and waved a final good-bye to our diminutive friend. Miraculously he understood and waved back. The gesture, I concluded, must have a double meaning in this culture.

As we walked the uneven sidewalk my feet began to ache, and I actually looked forward to our next encounter with the tube. It came soon enough. But this time the sleek metro car was not nearly so crowded. True, there still weren't any seats free, but at least we had sufficient room for falling down in the event of a lurch. I noticed that one elderly lady was even trying to read a comic book—though with only partial success.

Station followed station and we were soon above ground, racing along an elevated track in the middle of a busy motorway. An immense store, appropriately dubbed "Gigante," flashed past on one side. That was followed by a five-in-one movie theater advertising lurid titles. Then the usual array of small shops danced by like figures in a kinetoscope. A few moments later the track curved lazily to the left and we pulled into Tasqueña station—the end of the line. From there it was only a pleasant eight-block stroll through a park to Carbonera Street.

"This part of town is beautiful," I remarked as we barely avoided an aloe vera patch. "Open spaces and greenery! It's almost as though we were a million miles from that sooty beehive near the palace."

"Almost," Weston agreed while eyeing the high-tension wires overhead. "I wish every city would widen its traffic islands and turn them into gardens. There's just something about poplar trees and the fragrance of roses. Perhaps we're all still homesick for Eden."

I slowed down to check the map.

"That may be true," I reflected. "But homesick or not, we turn off at the next corner. Those houses over there certainly suffer from sameness, don't they? Why is it that cement boxes with picture windows are so much in vogue?"

"Because," Geoff rattled off, "concrete is plentiful, impervious to termites, a terrible insulator, and resistant to earthquakes. It's as solid as the middle class."

"And," I finished, "just as nondescript. Sometimes I wish there were no such thing as mass production."

"Old boy," Weston chided in a slightly mocking tone, "without the assembly line we wouldn't be where we are today."

I didn't answer. But as we turned onto the narrow residential lane, I wondered just where we were. Each dwelling rose two stories high and was neat as a pin. Colors alternated between white and pastel green—with occasional orange trim. Matchbook lawns sported lush green grass sliced off at the prescribed level. And every "crypt with a view" squatted securely behind its own tall, spiked fence. What a reversal of Genesis. We'd been allowed in the garden but were barred by steel slats from entering much of the land around it! My thoughts were interrupted as I tripped over a stump protruding from the sidewalk.

"Well, this is the right house number," Geoff remarked, then quipped, "I see you've stumbled onto the crime scene. Here you are already stumped and we haven't even started investigating."

"Oh, I don't know," I shot back in self-defense. "I rather fancy I was getting to the root of the matter." I rubbed my hands together to dust off the scrapes. "Do you really believe we'll find anything here? The locals, after all, are pretty well equipped for this kind of search."

Weston placed his hands on his hips and surveyed the street in both directions.

"I've no doubt that their procedures were adequate," he considered softly. "But I want the feel of the place. And I'm concerned about questions that Robledo may have forgotten to ask."

"Such as?"

"Let's assume the police discovered anything that might have been left behind by the kidnapper. Our goal will be determining what he took with him."

I scratched my head in consternation.

"And how, pray tell, shall we do that since what was taken isn't here?"

"Oh," Geoff disagreed, "but it is." He stooped down at the curb and pointed. "Take that blob of tar, for example. It's not inconceivable that the kidnapper stepped in it. Then there are prickly seeds in the grass, and I could go on and on. If we ever find the fellow, what's embedded in his shoe may convict him."

I slipped the magnifier out of my pocket and sank down to my hands and knees to begin work.

"I only hope," I commented, "that anything we turn up is distinctive enough so it will make a difference. Seeds—they're probably on every street within ten kilometers."

"It has to be enough." My partner's features hardened. "Did you notice any of the newspapers in the stands we passed downtown?"

I deposited a piece of broken glass in an evidence envelope.

"No. Why?"

"Because, old chap, there are too many murder suspects around here who have confessed on the front pages. God has given everyone a free will (no matter how corrupted it may be by sin), and I won't be party to an investigation that ends in a coerced admission of guilt. I'd rather see a kidnapper walk away free than to know he'd been dehumanized with a cattle prod."

"Surely," I protested, "you don't have to worry about anything like that happening. Inspector Robledo wouldn't—"

"No, he wouldn't order it. At least I don't think so. But men under him might become overzealous behind closed doors. Any case I put together has got to be airtight or I simply won't present the evidence."

"Which," I pointed out, "could jolly well get *you* in trouble."

"Indeed it could." Geoff compressed his lips grimly. "You take on the grass and sidewalk. I'll crawl around the gutter and street. Ah, my schoolteacher often said I'd end up in the gutter."

"Just see to it," I warned, "that you don't get flattened by a motorcar. We wouldn't want blood all over the clues." My gallows humor seemed to impress him not a whit.

We stopped talking and began casting about with the single-mindedness of hounds in search of the scent. Geoff almost literally kept his nose to the asphalt as he crisscrossed section after section of an imaginary grid. Nothing escaped his notice, and out of the corner of my eye I saw him stop several times to place tacks, paper, or chewing gum in a plastic bag. Crankcase oil likewise came in for a sampling. Meanwhile I worked my way from end to end along parallel lines examining stickers (most of which attached themselves to my knees), bits of glass, and manure donated to the city sod by philanthropic pets. The latter specimens, at least, had some chance of providing us with positive identification since they contained a wide range of chemicals. As the moments ticked by, drivers now and again slowed down to see what those balmy foreigners were up to. At such times I had to fight down an urge to call out something like: "Now where is that contact lens anyway?" We must have looked ridiculous exploring the land of Lilliput in our business suits.

When my last square foot was searched, I clambered to my feet and stretched the life back into protesting muscles. Geoff, I saw, was already sitting on the curb waiting for me.

"John, did you notice that no one in the homes around here appears to have seen us? Walls out front and elevated living rooms render us nearly invisible. I had wondered why any blighter would abandon a motorcar in so public a place, but now I realize it's not all that public."

"Except," I corrected, "for the presence of rubber-necked drivers."

"Who," Weston finished, "don't know what sedan goes with which house or particularly care. Now all we need to determine is why the Plymouth was dropped off so close to Memo's home. It's almost as if . . . " He snapped his fingers. "Yes, that's got to be it. Let's go pay our respects to Hernandez' relatives, and then we'll return to the palace to run a test or two."

San Francisco Street lay only two blocks north and turned out to be almost a carbon copy of Carbonera. It did, however, also contain a primary school complete with squealing boys playing soccer on the lawn. Memo's house was a good kick's distance farther east—a thirty yards or so that we traveled in near record time. I pushed the button mounted on the fence and we waited. Nothing happened.

"Perhaps," Weston speculated, "the bell's out of order." He cupped his hands like a megaphone. "Hola, in there! We are detectives here to help!"

That did it! The door swung open and an elderly lady in a shawl came creaking toward us. She had high cheeks, a broad, blunt nose, and salt and pepper hair pulled back tightly in a bun. But she wasn't wearing a smile.

"What is the meaning of shouting that out for the whole neighborhood, señor?" Her voice quavered. "We would just as soon keep our business to ourselves." As she approached and stopped on the other side of the fence, I could see that her arms were shaking as well. I guessed she was the grandmother.

"Pardóneme, por favor." Geoff tried to smooth things over. "Apparently your chimes were not working."

"Oh," she scolded, "yes, they were. But no one ever waits a decent interval anymore to give a woman a chance to come outside. Much pleasure in knowing you." Her tone was perfunctory. "Now, what do you want?"

I shook my head in wonder at the woman's pluck. She was a real firebrand.

"We would like," I explained, "to speak with as many members of the family as possible about Memo. We want to get a feeling for his personality."

"No, you don't." The abuela stared straight at me through her bloodshot eyes. "He was a horrible boy. Always throwing things around or lying in bed letting his brothers run errands. And secretive! Since he started work in the palace, he's been too good even to talk to us. I remember when he was so nice and considerate, too. When he was a little boy he sold newspapers and gave everything to—"

"That's very interesting," I interrupted. "But is there anyone else home? We'd like to interview as many people as possible."

"You don't want to talk to me." She seemed disappointed. "No one ever does."

"That is not the case," Geoff stepped in. "But we would like a whole series of impressions. I don't suppose anyone else is home?"

Our matronly host shook her head.

"Not except for Ceci. She has only two years of age, but already she says 'Papa . . . carro' when she wants to go out with the family. You have never seen a smarter girl in your life! Just last week—"

"I'm sure," Geoff agreed, "that she's an extraordinary young lady. And it's pleasant to pass time chatting with you. Mature women like yourself have so much to give to the family, don't you think? You train up children to appreciate their heritage."

The abuela's wrinkled cheeks made room for a smile.

"Yes," she declared, "I guess I do. I mean, I do, don't I? You may only be tossing flowers my way to butter me up, but what you say is true."

Weston removed a business card from his pocket and penciled in a phone number.

"When the family arrives," he requested, "will you please give them this and tell them I would very much appreciate it if they would ring us up?"

"Claro que sí." The woman accepted the card through the bars. "I'll do it as soon as they come. Have a nice day."

"The same to you."

We turned away from the fence and began retracing our steps toward the trains and the stained-glass windows of Tasqueña station. I breathed deep draughts of good air as we walked—preparing for the stuffy closeness on the Metro. And I wondered what the terrible knowledge was that had cost Memo Hernandez his freedom. The trip home proved uneventful.

Chapter 3

The Kidnap Nap

It had been a long day. And the western sky glowed with reddish orange streaks when I looked up at last from the microfiche viewer. I felt washed out—numb above the neck. But at least we had one more tiny bit of information. I leaned back in the chair, interlocked my hands behind my head, and gazed listlessly across the room at Geoff. He was still bent over the microscope studying soil samples.

"When Hernandez' father called," I remarked, "he didn't perchance say his son was addicted to Fiestas, did he?"

"No," Weston replied offhandedly. "To Kents. So we now know the kidnapper's taste in cigarette poison."

"It would seem so," I reflected, "unless the gentleman lit up with matches or our chemical composition charts have become outdated. How are you coming with the soils?"

My partner paused to rub his eye.

"Not very well, I'm afraid. Those floorboards must have been collecting mud for several years. So far I've isolated ten different kinds and there's no end in sight."

"Which means," I sighed, "we've hit a dead end."

"That's about it," Weston admitted uneasily. "Dirt from the attacker's shoe isn't going to lead us to his hideout. And even if the stuff's in our envelopes, it won't be all that useable as evidence once he's found."

"So where do we go from here?"

"That," my partner concluded, "is a rattling good question." He got to his feet and began his usual pacing back and forth. "I suppose we could run over *all* the ground again that the locals have covered. But I for one would hate to interrogate an entire parade of Memo's friends. What's more, I doubt I'd even know the right questions to ask. The problem with this case is that it's too simple. Devastatingly simple!"

I raised my eyebrows a notch. "But surely there's at least the matter of where the motorcar was dropped off. I for one find that highly irregular."

Geoff stroked his goatee in thought.

"Yes," he reflected, "that does open up one or two interesting possibilities. Beginning with the obvious, it tells us the kidnappers knew where their victim lived. Remind me to have Robledo find out if any neighbors saw someone spying on Hernandez' house."

"I'll try to remember. Now, what about the less obvious? *Why* did they abandon it where they did?"

"Perhaps," Weston surmised, "they wanted us to believe he disappeared voluntarily and had simply left the motorcar where he was sure his parents would eventually find it."

I shook my head. "You've got to do better than that! From what we've heard about Memo, that kind of generosity would hardly be in character."

"Unless," Geoff amended, "they thought we'd assume he was planning to return and wanted his family to take care of the Plymouth in the interim. Remember that Porfirio must have been convinced of some such motive until we showed him the scratch on the ceiling. But, I'll grant you, the theory's somewhat weak. I'm inclined to believe the kidnappers simply wanted everyone to suppose Guillermo was abducted near home by neighborhood bully boys."

"But that," I objected, "would mean—"

"Precisely. We wouldn't consider that story for a minute if we knew about Memo's inside information. So they must have assumed we wouldn't know."

I closed my eyes and sighed.

"You have at least succeeded in complicating matters. But I don't see we're any nearer a solution. We already knew the blighters weren't omniscient."

"Yes, of course."

Geoff stopped pacing and ran his fingers through his hair.

"I feel positively dull today, John. Perhaps we should have taken time out for a decent lunch and a siesta. If we could even get away for a few hours."

"There's a concert tonight at Bellas Artes," I suggested brightly—cheered at the thought of playing tourist. "One of the guards mentioned it would be worth attending."

"That," my partner enthused, "is just the thing! And after the concert we'll stop in at a good restaurant for supper. Tomorrow's a new day, and we're going to enter it with recharged batteries and a fresh outlook on the case. Besides," he added ruefully, "there's nothing more we can do tonight. We're completely out of leads."

I buttoned the top button of my shirt and looked around for my tie. For the first time since our arrival in Mexico I wished that Jane Albey were in the city. (Not that I would word it quite like that to her! She is very patient with our sometimes-erratic social life, but I wouldn't want her to think, "out of sight, out of mind.") She would have enjoyed the symphony here.

*   *   *   *   *

The musty odor of sewer gas hung over the trees, benches, and fountains as Weston and I climbed the last few steps out of Bellas Artes tube station. We had emerged in the midst of an inner city forest! Five-globed street lights cast a warm glow over enamorados walking arm in arm. And water danced like liquid fire about the knees of marble nymphs bathing in seething pools. After turning around like open-mouthed tourists, Geoff and I headed along a broad sidewalk toward the edge of the park. The concert hall lay just beyond.

"This," I remarked as we walked, "is a lovely change of pace. I believe I'd rather be here than under the spreading branches of Lothlorien."

"Except," Geoff glanced in distaste at a large bronze statue, "that in Tolkien's world we wouldn't be subjected to an occasional sculpted monstrosity."

I craned my neck to see what we'd passed.

"Why, I think it's rather good, really. A naked wrestler gripping the legs of an angel. Though I don't imagine Jacob was quite that muscular."

Weston looked down his nose at me. "John, you didn't notice the caption. The hunk of metal is entitled 'Beethoven.' "

"Beethoven! You must be joking."

"I wish I were. I wonder what Ludwig would think to see himself portrayed like that."

"Either," I concluded, "that our sense of history's off or our sense of propriety."

"He's certainly not your average angel wrestler," Geoff agreed. "Now if he were at the feet of Rousseau, that I could believe!"

We dodged traffic across a street and skirted the wall of the concert hall in search of an entrance. As we walked, stone heads looked down at us from above locked doors and deserted balconies. Marble maidens in flowing robes peeked from behind columns, and mountaineering angels helped naked human comrades over the crest of the roof. The building seemed busy even when it was empty! High above us on the top of the dome more unclothed statues held hands and danced around—what else—an eagle with a snake in its beak.

Weston remarked, "Look at the arch over the front door. In spite of the cherubs in the background, the scene is decidedly sensual. So this is the Palace of the Beautiful Arts! Let's hope the orchestra inside is featuring something soft, dignified, and traditional. I'd like to relax and close my eyes for a few moments."

"You and I both!"

We passed through the portals into an anteroom of swirled pink, brown, and green marble cut to exacting straight lines and clean symmetry. It was as though we'd advanced two centuries. The soft round columns outside gave way to square. And the neo-classical statuary was replaced by modernistic gargoyles and wall-length murals painted by heavy-handed Latin moderns. Each balcony up served as another geometric picture frame. As we stood in line to buy our tickets, I simply gawked. At the back of the room a half flight up, massive chrome doors topped by a bronze theatrical mask marked the entrance to the auditorium's first floor. But marble stairs spread upward like wings from its sides. And on the ground level, alcoves served as galleries filled with poster-like art nouveau. I let out a low whistle. "Geoff, we've got a couple of moments before curtain. Why don't we take a look around?"

My partner picked up the tickets through the window.

"That, old bean, has already been arranged. The only seats left are in the second balcony. We'll see murals on the way until our eyes pop out."

Geoff and I followed the crowd toward the doors and then peeled off to climb the first flight. At the head of the stairs we paused briefly to try to figure out something called "Mexico of Today." We failed. Solid flames, spare tires, and surrealistic "people" conveyed more about the artist's struggle for meaning than about any meaning he'd found. On the third level we hardly slowed as we walked by women and men turned grotesque, big boned and harsh by an artist criticizing what he called "The New Democracy." As we turned the corner, however, both Weston and I came to a sudden standstill.

"Now there," Geoff breathed, "is a truly dangerous painting. The artist is a genius."

The mural spread before us in all its complexity. On the left a benevolent Darwin tended his pet monkeys in front of a bloodless, broken-armed statue of an evil philosopher—wearing a crucifix. Behind him bug-eyed soldiers in gas masks marched against the crowds. Another bloodless statue stood to the right—decapitated but clutching a swastika. At its feet Engles, Marx and Trotsky sat as ruddy-cheeked gentlemen instructing the masses while an army of peasants, waving red flags, marched by. And in the center between these two extremes stood deified, omnipotent man—a Russian worker holding an atom in the grasp of a hand turned half machine! Electrons buzzed in orbits about him, forming butterfly wings on which were etched suns and microscopes and all the scientific achievements of man. To the left idle capitalists turned their backs and drank martinis, but to the right a dignified Lenin looked on approvingly.

"That," I observed, "is the neatest piece of communist propaganda I've ever seen."

"It is, isn't it?" Weston concurred. "The wonder is that Diego Rivera was actually paid for it by representatives of a capitalistic state! His technique is so good that he makes lies look appealing and spits in the face of the viewer without the person even being aware of it. To achieve this, he's borrowed from nearly everybody I can think of—from Renoir and Cezánne to Boticelli and Michaelangelo, with a dash of

Byzantine fresco thrown in for good measure."

"He certainly is a master at charging a canvas with emotion," I agreed.

Geoff pointed to the cocktail party.

"Not only that," he observed, "but at slanting the emotion. Look how ugly those women are! And they're the only capitalists even painted as human. The others are all bugs or statues! Notice also how he subtly uses color to enhance or detract. Communists are in technicolor. Everyone else is drab or pale."

"What an instrument for devilry!" I shook my head. "If a man writes an essay, he can be rebutted and proven a fool. But if he produces a work of art, no one quite knows how to respond."

"Because," Weston continued, "he's created a fantasy land rather than a statement of propositional truth. The correct way to rebut would, I suppose, be to take up one's own paintbrush. But, unfortunately, Christian artists are a minority and usually not very good. So we see man proclaimed a monkey and the monkey made god without an answering volley from our side."

The discordant sounds of the orchestra tuning up caught our attention from the auditorium. I sighed and took the lead as we hurried down the outside balcony toward the open door.

"Wouldn't it be nice," I whispered just before we entered, "if evangelicals took to the offensive with art. A medium with that kind of power shouldn't be ignored."

"Wouldn't it!" Geoff chuckled under his breath. "Imagine an atheist admiring a Christian painting in spite of himself!"

We were handed our programs as we passed through the entrance, but the house lights began to dim before I could so much as read a line. We'd hardly taken our seats when the baton was raised and the orchestra struck two distinctive chords. I smiled to myself. The opening selection was Brahms' Tragic Overture. Soft waves of melody began lapping from wall to wall—rising in force ever so gradually until they enveloped the room. I closed my eyes and floated serenly from crest to crest. Ever so slowly the day's tension and fatigue drained away. Mozart followed Brahms. Then came the flow and ebb of a waltz by my late friend Robert Stoltz. A little over half-way through, I heard a faint murmuring in the seat next to me. Geoff was snoring. I let him doze on until the crystal curtain came down, signaling the end of the performance.

We left the concert hall reluctantly—still savoring the infinite variation of themes. Outside, horns honked and hoarse-voiced cabbies yelled "taxi" at the top of their lungs. We ignored the cacophony, however, and walked toward the palace while at the same time checking the street for restaurants. Finally we hit upon one. But, oh, what a name! I looked in the window apprehensively.

"Geoff, I don't know. Can any good thing come out of 'Burger Baby'?"

My partner held the door open for me with a flourish.

"There's only one way to find out, old chap. Live dangerously."

We stepped inside, ordered at the fast-food counter, and thanked the Lord while we waited. It turned out to be an interesting meal. The chillied carrots and onions cleared out our sinuses and the scrambled eggs satisfied our appetites. The ham aroused our curiosity. We wondered how meat could be sliced so thin that light shone through it. A glass of milk, orange juice, and a cup of coffee completed the dinner menu #1 and more than quenched our thirst.

Since it was only a few blocks from the Burger Baby to the National Palace, we decided to continue on foot. The evening was pleasant. Traffic had lightened to the point that the air was tolerable. And the sidewalks were well lit. We made good time and arrived home by eleven. Within half an hour both of us were sound asleep, dreaming about chillied atoms, radioactive carrots, and a man who was lauded for making a monkey out of himself.

* * * * *

As I fought my way back to consciousness, I was dimly aware that my temples were throbbing in tune with my pulse. And the pit of my stomach was sending out queasy signals I couldn't ignore much longer. On a happier note, the enticing aroma of freshly brewed tea was drifting in from the living room. I had a choice. I could remain snuggly under the warm covers groaning softly to myself, or I could grab my clothes, make a mad dash across icy floors to the lavatory and prepare to face another morning. Like a swimmer testing the water, I gingerly slid one leg over the side of the bed and touched the tile with a toe. I shuddered. Well, I might as well get it over with. I tossed my blankets in the air and ran.

It's amazing the difference a wash and a shave can make. By the time I stepped into the living room I felt almost human—though a trifle weak. Geoff, seated at a folding table he'd dug out of the closet, appeared slightly green around the gills.

"Well," I greeted him ruefully, "we lived dangerously."

My partner ignored the statement and poured a second cup.

"Have some tea, John. It's just the thing to settle your stomach." He added a dash of lemon and set the steaming brew down in front of my chair. "I'm sorry I can't offer you any crumpets, but the cupboard does have its limitations. I was fortunate to find even a cooker. This place is not exactly—"

There was a loud, urgent knock at the door.

"Mr. Weston, are you in there?" The voice was muffled, but the peremtory tone was unmistakable. "Mr. Taylor— Mr. Weston, will you come immediately before I have someone beat the door down, por favor?" Since his perfunctory "please" did nothing to move the statement from threat to request, I hurried to the entrance and unbolted the latch. "Sí, Señor, un momento, por favor!" (I was not going to answer in kind.)

Geoff wasn't more than a step behind me when the door burst inward and a round-faced gentleman in a pin-striped suit strode in as though spearheading an invasion. Two sentries stood at attention behind him on the balcony.

"Have you seen him? Is he here?" Our mustached visitor looked keenly at the open doorways.

"It might help," Geoff informed him politely, "if you would tell us, Mr. President, whom you are seeking."

"My son, Señor! My son! Have you seen him?" Augustin Guerrero had had a politician's practice in concealing emotion, but his voice cracked with the raw edge of panic.

Geoff put his arm around the dignitary's shoulders.

"No, Señor, we have not heard from Salvador since yesterday. But if you will confide in us we may be able to help. Here is some tea brewed if—"

"Gracias. I believe I will join you." Guerrero brushed past us. "This whole thing is so incredible, I can't believe it is happening. Perhaps consultations would help."

"That," I assured him, "is what we are here for." Smiling and shrugging like a true Mexican, I closed the door on the soldiers and followed Geoff and our guest to the table. As they settled down, I pulled up an extra chair and poured a third cup.

"Now," Weston opened warmly, "tell us the particulars."

Augustin sipped the steaming liquid and grimaced as though it were medicine.

"Mr. Weston, Salvador wasn't here when I arrived this morning. That's not unusual. He often leaves early for work, so I didn't think anything of it. But the bank just called asking if he would be in today. La policía militar has searched virtually everywhere and he's not in the palace. But the guards on duty say he never left. He was here last night. He's gone this morning. And nobody knows the why or the how."

"That," Geoff sympathized, "would seem to be unusual. The guards, I assume, were stationed in pairs."

"Sí. And they are beyond suspicion. I'm afraid the hand that snatched away my son's friend has now reached into this very building for him!" Given the circumstances, I didn't feel his estimation was unduly dramatic.

Weston brooded over his cup, considering the implications. "I believe," he concluded soberly, "that there are several steps which must be taken immediately. You are concerned, and rightfully so, about your son's disappearance. But if what you say is true, everyone in this building is in danger. There's a security gap here that must be closed before two or three others turn up missing. I suggest that every key worker be given a bodyguard at once. You might also plug all telephone lines into recording and tracing devices. We have to assume a kidnapping. If that's so, you should be hearing from the abductors before too long."

"Done!" Augustin declared, relieved at having a commission. Tea sloshed as he pounded on the table. "What else can we do?"

"You could," I ventured, "give us an hour or so in Salvador's apartment to search for clues."

"Before," Geoff amended, "the police . . . uh, are called. I would also like an interview with any of your son's brothers or sisters who might be available. The generation gap being what it is, sometimes siblings know crucial facts parents never suspect."

"You think my—"

"I think nothing," Weston cut him off. "It's my job to investigate. And part of that process involves determining motive. Why was Salvador the target, for instance? Why not you? I need to know your son inside out in order to help him. I also need to be fully acquainted with this building. Will you grant us a free hand to stick our noses into every corner?"

The President's face remained impassive.

"Within limits, Mr. Weston. Certain offices are, of necessity, restricted."

"I see." My partner held our visitor in a steady gaze. "Do I have your word that there are no secret escape tunnels from the palace—tunnels designed for use in the event of mass rioting or a coup attempt?"

"You do not," Augustin admitted. "There is such a tunnel, but I can't disclose its location to you or to anyone else. Only a handful even know of its existence."

"Including," I asked, "your son?"

"Yes. But even if he had told someone else about it—which thing he would never do—the information would be useless."

"How so?" Weston prompted.

The President folded his hands and fought for calmness.

"Because there are five doors in the tunnel that can be opened only from the *inside*. And even then one must know their combination—a sequence changed every month. Salvador did not have that information. Only department heads do. The tunnel is secure, my friend. It was not used in the kidnapping."

"I see." Weston stroked his beard thoughtfully. "I noticed a freight-elevator grating in the sidewalk out front. Is there a chance—?"

"That too," Augustin interrupted, "is operable only from within. And the padlock on the inner door hasn't been touched. I've already checked."

"You are," Geoff admired, "most thorough. We shall attempt to be, as well, if you would be good enough to have a soldier escort us to Salvador's apartment."

"Yes, of course." Augustin rose to his feet and we followed his lead.

"You might also," I suggested as we headed for the exit, "ring up Inspector Robledo and tell him of the new developments. He will, no doubt, wish to take certain measures himself. A good man, the Inspector," I added with a sidelong glance at our host.

We parted from Augustin outside the apartment and accompanied one of the military policemen along the third-level walkway rimming the courtyard. As we did, I viewed the ancient walls with renewed interest. They were porous enough and had sufficient ledges to be enticing to a cat burglar. The green wrought-iron railings bordering the balconies contained filigree work that would easily anchor a climbing rope. Only the three-foot glass overhang at roof level posed a real problem to someone descending from above. Getting inside, I decided, might not be impossible even with the large complement of guards on hand. But dragging someone else out would be a decidedly sticky wicket.

Our uniformed companion stopped four doors down from our apartment and worked a key in the latch. Without saying a word, he then stood to one side and allowed us to enter. By the time the door clicked closed behind us, his rifle was off his shoulder and in position to defend us against the unknown. We, it appeared, were the first to receive a bodyguard.

I surveyed our client's quarters with an eye for detail. The floors were covered with an oriental rug whose reds and blues were just as mellow as the day they'd come off the loom. The easy chair and sofa likewise reeked with a plush newness. And the writing desk, concert grand piano and coffee table were of dark, unscratched mahogany. I had a feeling we'd walked into a furniture showroom rather than an apartment. The place hardly looked lived in. There wasn't so much as a yellow streak in the wallpaper, and the window overlooking Emiliano Zapata Street sparkled.

"What elegance," Geoff commented. "One can almost smell the factory odor. Well, at least we won't have to sift through two inches of dust and discarded newspapers. You concentrate on the left side of the room. I'll take the right. That roll-top desk and bookcase are too much to resist."

"First," I corrected, "I'll give the carpet a going over. Let's remove our shoes so we don't end up convicting ourselves."

Weston stopped and began unlacing.

"Quite so. That must be the kitchen off to the left—I assume he has a kitchen. It would be dreadful living here for an extended period without one. And the bedroom must be to the rear. It's almost the same floor plan we have in our quarters."

"Except," I complained, "that his cooking area is your bedroom and we are forced to patronize Burger Baby." I knelt down and began crawling over the rug—clearing a strip for Geoff's feet. But after completing a sweep down and back, nothing significant had come under my lens.

"One thing is certain about our client," I observed. "He didn't spend much time at home. Either that or he redecorates every month. The pile isn't even mashed down."

"Perhaps," Geoff encouraged, "you'll find a bit more wear toward the center in a traffic lane." He walked my narrow strip to the desk, put on white gloves, and set to work rummaging in the pigeon holes.

The carpet continued to be rich in color but poverty stricken in clues. I had the feeling as I worked that my pant legs were leaving more traces of human habitation behind than my magnifier was picking up. Row followed row and I finally reached the rug's edge empty-handed. When I looked up, I noticed the perplexed frown on Weston's face. He didn't seem to be faring any better than I. A pile of papers, boxes, and rubber stamps was growing on the desk's writing area as he emptied drawers piece by piece, but the pieces were ordinary—exactly what one would expect to find.

I began to inspect my side by opening the wardrobe in the corner by the front door. All it contained was a jacket, an umbrella, and two greatcoats. The jacket was slightly worn. I turned to it first and started going through the pockets.

"Uh-oh!" My hand closed around a pack of cigarettes. Even before lifting them out, I had a sneaking suspicion. "Here are the Fiestas," I grimaced while holding them aloft for Geoff to see. "It looks like the lighter was a dead end."

"Not necessarily," my partner disagreed. "Check the cellophane for prints. Those may not be Salvador's cigarettes. Even if they are, it's a popular brand. Someone besides our client may have lighted up in Memo's motorcar." He went back to his patient search of a drawer.

I patted my own pockets for the fingerprint kit and then put it to use. Brushing powder off the thin plastic, I found a single perfect thumb print which I routinely transferred to tape and marked with an identifying note. Then it was on to examining the rest of the wardrobe. All I came up with were two buttons, a pen, a laundry receipt, and a thimbleful of lint.

The piano bench was next on my tour, but it only revealed that our client enjoyed jazz. The piano itself was immaculate. There wasn't even any dust on the hammer felt. Two end tables contained an assortment of financial magazines and nothing else.

As a matter of routine, but without any great sense of expectation, I began dispensing powder over the furniture. The tables were clean. The wood trim on the sofa yielded a badly smudged print. And there were three on the piano keys. Comparing all five under the glass, I came to the conclusion that they belonged to the same person. That almost certainly meant they were Salvador's. I'd just begun extracting loose change from behind the cushions when there was a thud behind me. Geoff had dropped one of the drawers on the floor and was groping in the recess of the desk.

"I hope it's not a Chippendale," I reproved. "You're beginning to acquire the Yard's touch."

"Neither Chippendale nor chipped," Weston assured me with a grin. "It's a good copy though. What ho! Now what do we have here?" He brought his hand out of the cavity holding a single folded slip of paper. "This would seem to have fallen behind when the drawer overflowed. Or it could have been placed there for safe keeping. Let's see if it's anything significant." He opened up the sheet and pondered its contents.

"John, come have a look at this. What do you make of it?"

I ambled over and scanned the paper.

A las siete
131C Heroes de Nacozari
Alma y Irma me enviaron

"Well," I ventured after consulting my map, "the address is about nine blocks northeast of here. And it's almost certainly an apartment judging from the 'C' in the house number."

"That much," Weston acknowledged impatiently, "is obvious. But what can you tell me of the writer."

"From the backward slant of the letters," I considered, "he's probably a left-hander."

Geoff raised his eyebrows.

"He?"

"He." I defended myself. "A woman wouldn't use that bold, boxy style. At least I don't think so. It must have been a man . . . probably one in a hurry."

"Not only in a hurry," my partner added with satisfaction, "but semi-literate in Spanish. The chap was also probably sick."

I looked at the note again to see what I'd missed.

"How in the world do you conclude that? If the address were written quickly on a moving metro car it would—"

"Then," Geoff agreed, "we could account for the shaky lines. But that wouldn't explain the grammar and spelling errors. Notice there's no accent over the 'e' in Héroes. The word order's wrong. And, even more significantly, the word 'y' rather than 'e' is used before 'Irma.' No Mexican—not even a poorly educated one—would say Alma *y* Irma."

"Then you suspect?"

"I'm absolutely certain," Weston declared solemnly. "Salvador had a rendezvous with a foreigner. A meeting so secret that he had to give a code signal to get him in the door! And it couldn't have been that long ago, either. The paper's crisp, and the dated material in the drawer isn't more than a few months old."

I whistled softly.

"Things are starting to look bleak for our client, aren't they? Inspector Robledo may have been right about a staged kidnapping. Just wrong about who was doing the staging."

"That," my partner nodded, "is a distinct possibility. If Salvador were a traitor, it *would* explain the Fiesta ashes in Memo's motorcar. Salvador might have silenced his friend or used him as a scapegoat. On the other hand, I hate to think the worst of a client. He did, after all, pay a small fortune for his bodyguard's return."

"Which," I pointed out, "could have been a diversion."

"Yes, it could." Geoff drummed his fingers on the desk top. "But if he had a scapegoat and had successfully diverted suspicion, why would he disappear? He'd have no reason to. No, I believe events here are deeper than meet the eye." He paused to stuff the note into an evidence envelope and seal it up. "We'll have to reserve judgment until we've visited 131C Héroes de Nacozari. For now, let's concentrate on the rest of this apartment."

Weston bent down and pulled the rest of the drawers out of their tracks. However, no other notes were to be seen. I abandoned being a spectator and returned to the job of searching cushions. For my pains I found a stick of chewing gum, two five peso pieces, and a comb. By the time I'd finished, Geoff was about through scanning the bookcase.

"There's nothing over this way," I reported. "What about you, old chap? Does our 'victim' fill his mind with spy stories?"

Weston's eyes never wavered from the titles as he answered. "Not in the least. He seems to favor books on economics, medicine, health foods, flying saucers, and dream analysis. In short, the man's got both a serious and a sensationalistic side to his nature. But there's nothing incriminating . . . unless he's in league with Martians planning to turn us all into organic vegetables. Speaking of food, why don't you have a quick look around the kitchen. Be sure to dust the refrigerator door handle and the light switch."

"While I'm at it," I added, "I'll inspect every switch plate, window latch, and doorknob in the house. Come to think of it, we should have stopped that soldier before he touched the outside latch. We're not at our sharpest this morning at all."

"No," Geoff admitted, "we're not. But an off day every

now and then is to be expected. When you've finished, you'll find me in the bedroom."

I set about fingerprinting all of those places that hands are most likely to contact. There was a smudge here, a partial there, and a full print every so often. All appeared to be Salvador's. After fifteen minutes I had discovered only that the living-room window was locked from the inside and the icebox might as well have been. Pickled seaweed didn't tempt me in the slightest.

As I stepped through the doorway into the bedroom, I instantly noticed a change. This was the inner sanctum where our client could cast off his banker image and be human like the rest of us. Magazines lay askew on top of the tele, the bed was unmade, and everything from cuff links to cologne had been strewn across the dresser. My first thought was to check the window. It, too, I found was locked and there were no prints. About that time Geoff emerged from the closet carrying an empty hanger.

"This," he volunteered, "is all that's left of the suit we saw Salvador wearing the first night. It's either at the cleaners or on his back."

"In which case," I pointed out, "he was hardly dragged out in his nightshirt."

In answer Weston walked over to the dresser and pulled open the top drawer. There was a whole pile of neatly stacked pajamas inside.

"John, I'm not sure but that he may have been. The young man would hardly have that many pairs of pajamas if he didn't use them. But there isn't any wrinkled discard from last night lying around."

"Perhaps," I suggested facetiously, "he wore the one over the other."

"Or, more probably, his abductors didn't have time to dress him but grabbed a suit off the rack for future use. I've about finished here, but I would like you to dust the face of the tele and the remote tuner on the night table. If he was watching a movie when the kidnappers arrived, they might have been the ones who shut it off."

"With," I reminded him, "the same gloved hands that didn't leave a mark on any doorknobs." I set about testing the face of the television first. "Shall I check the inside for elf prints as well? The little rascals may have hid under the picture tube, you know, and come out at night to vaporize."

"That," Weston smiled, "won't be necessary. I've already taken the back off and had a peek. Neither sleeping gas nor elfen cots are in evidence. Nor do the rabbit ears reach out to strangle the unwary."

"And neither are there any fingerprints on the front," I informed him a moment later. "Our client must have used the remote button almost exclusively." I straightened up and stretched the kinks out of my back. "Face it, Geoff. There's no physical evidence that any blighters broke in or that they even knew Salvador had valuable information. If they—"

"That's it!" Weston slammed his fist into his palm. "How could they know! I'm going to look in the tele again. You remove the face plates from the wall outlets and switches. And tear apart that bed. I think this place is bugged."

"After I dust the control unit," I amended stubbornly.

White powder on the dark plastic brought out a number of prints. But it was the same old story. They all belonged to the President's son. He must have *never* invited visitors into the apartment! I slid my kit back into my pocket and looked about for something useable as a screwdriver. A nail file on the dresser looked like it would do nicely.

The wall outlets opened up before my assault like so many oysters, but if I'd been a pearl diver I would have starved to death. One by one they turned up empty. So I pulled the mattress off the bed and started inspecting the springs.

"Here it is," I breathed in triumph, "wrapped around a coil right under the chap's pillow. The whole bed was a transmitting antenna."

Weston wedged the back onto the tele and came over for a closer look. As he crouched down, his eyelids narrowed to slits.

"My word, they certainly used plenty of power. That set has a range of a couple of miles."

"So much," I concluded, "for tracing them down with a house-to-house search. Do you suppose they've overheard our conversation?"

Geoff bit his lip as he mulled over the possibility. "I don't think so. They shouldn't have any reason to monitor the broadcast now that they have their victim. But then again, why didn't they remove the bug last night when they had the chance? Turn the thing off and wrap it up. I'm going to make a call."

As I disconnected the antenna, he stepped over to the bedside table, picked up the telephone receiver and dialed zero.

"Bueno. Please connect me with the President immediately. No, I'm not joking. Tell him Mr. Weston has an urgent communication. Yes. W-E-S-T-O-N. He'll know who I am. Of course I'll hold." He started pacing back and forth, stretching the cord like a tethered horse itching to be free. "Yes, Mr. President, it's I again. I have a crucial question to ask you and. . . . No, there's nothing classified involved. I need to know if you or the secret police have planted listening devices in your son's quarters. Yes, I'm completely serious. I understand. Then we'll have to make a mad dash to follow up a lead. Please give the Inspector a message for us. Tell him to search the living room here for other microphones. While he's at it, I'd like our own quarters searched . . . and your offices as well. Also have him inspect this building's sewer system and the roofs. Yes, the roofs. Someone might have shot a rope over from across the street. If so, there may be scratches left by the anchor. Oh, yes, there's one more thing. Could you have a taxi waiting at the front entrance within the next two minutes? No, I don't want a limousine. A taxi will be fine. Thank you. Good day." My partner slammed the receiver down into its cradle and started for the door.

"John, run as you've never run before. If there were eavesdroppers, we've got to get to Héroes de Nacozari Street before they can react. If we're too late, we may find an empty house or, worse yet, a group of dead conspirators. For all we know there may be more than one nest of spies!"

By the time I'd stuffed the deactivated transmitter into my coat pocket, Geoff was halfway across the living room. I took his advice and sprinted toward the door!

Chapter 4

Weston and the Devil's Den

Our taxi sped along sidewalks jammed with people who swarmed through a world of pock-marked walls, marred by chipped and fading paint. Hand-lettered shop signs hung over narrow stalls. Potted plants clung tenaciously to rusted wrought iron window decorations. Empty lots stood paved by the rubble of tenements hit by too many earthquakes. Our cabbie leaned on his horn repeatedly as individuals broke away from the crowded sidewalks and darted in front of our motorcar. Flies hovered over a fruit stand as we passed; the rancid odor of overripe mangoes made me nauseous.

"It's hard to visualize our dapper client in this neighborhood," I admitted wonderingly. "Somehow I'd expected a more middle-class meeting."

"You and I both," Geoff agreed. "About now I wish we had a couple of Webleys with us. Thanks to the police, I'm not even carrying my pocket knife."

"We could always stop and call Porfirio."

"And perhaps ruin the Guerrero family in the process." Weston shook his head resolutely. "No, John. We don't *know* that Salvador's a traitor. We don't know *why* he set up the rendezvous. And we can't tell anyone our suspicions until they're confirmed or disproven by the facts. You and I will simply have to peek in a few windows and then decide on a course of action. We may, as it were, walk into the lion's den and depend on the Lord for protection."

"Ya llegamos," our driver announced. He veered toward the curb and braked to a screeching stop. "That will be fourteen pesos."

Weston handed a bill forward and switched to Spanish. "Here's a fifty. Keep driving around the block until you hear from us. If the account goes higher than that, we'll pay the difference."

The cabbie stuffed the money in his shirt with an air of boredom.

"As you wish, Señor. There are too many cars going by for me to get out and open the door."

Taking the hint I jerked the handle and we stepped out on the sidewalk in front of one of the most dismal buildings on the street. The instant I slammed the door, the motorcar accelerated, raced into the flow of traffic, and left us very much alone. "Lord," I prayed under my breath, "we're here on a mission of justice. Please close the lion's mouth."

The building was constructed of gray, sooty lava blocks. Two hundred years ago it may have housed government offices. Now the drive-through gate was nailed closed and a small splintered door had been hacked out at its center. Hinges had decayed. The tiny door canted to one side and was barely more than a piece of scrap leaning against the mouth of an alley. Inside I could make out a dark passage, lined with butane tanks and trash, that led to a courtyard.

Geoff nodded his satisfaction. "There are so many clotheslines at the end of that tunnel, old bean, that I think we have a chance of approaching unnoticed. It's good we came on wash day."

I nodded soberly, then bent down to keep from bumping my head as I stepped inside. Dank chill air touched my face and water dripped noisily from pipes overhead. We cautiously shuffled forward over the wet, slimy, stone surface.

"Here's hoping," I whispered, "we don't have to leave on the run." My voice sounded hoarse and hollow—louder than I'd intended.

The courtyard, when we reached it, was somewhat of an improvement. Through the jungle of ropes and dingy underwear in the sunshine, we could make out four screen doors—each with a letter tacked to its rotting frame. Next to every door there was a single dirty window almost as opaque as the powdery wall. Judging from the laundry hanging in front of apartment C, several men and woman and at least two children were in residence. Battered jeans seemed to be standard dress for both sexes.

"This does not look like the average spy nest," Geoff observed raspily. "Let's take off our jackets and shirts so we fit in a little better. Then I'm going to clean their window for them."

"You'll also pay the cleaning bills for our suits," I threatened as I stripped off my shirt. "Oh my. I'll fit in better than I dreamed. There's a hole in my undershirt." I wrapped up our discards and laid them next to a wall in the shadow of the tunnel. Geoff threw his wallet on top of the pile and motioned me to do the same.

"Really," I whined, "this is too much. What are the chances they'll be here when we get back?"

"A mite better than ours," Weston observed, "if we're searched and they find our business cards." He added his watch and belt to the pile. Reluctantly I followed his lead.

The two of us tiptoed toward the right-hand wall—keeping as much laundry between us and the window as possible. Once at the wall we worked our way along until we were right next to the window of apartment C. A dull murmuring came from inside, barely audible over the sound of my heartbeat. Geoff rubbed a quarter-sized hole in the window dirt with his finger and put his eye to the glass for a lingering moment. Then he quickly backed away and rejoined me. He motioned with his head and the two of us retraced our steps to the privacy of the tunnel.

"Well," I whispered with barely concealed excitement, "what did you see?"

My partner paused for an infuriatingly long second.

"I saw," he mused with considerable puzzlement, "a hippy commune. There were, I believe, four young men and about twice as many girls—probably Americans. At the moment they're sitting on the floor, contemplating their navels and smoking breakfast. I've seen more intelligent eyes on fish."

"Then they're not spies?"

"I hardly think so . . . unless the spy business has gone to pot." Geoff scratched his chin. "I rather fancy we've stumbled onto the state secret Salvador was so bent on protecting."

"But that's preposterous! What's so important about a commune that—"

"Salvador attended drug parties," Weston interrupted.

"If knowledge of that got out, what would it do to his father's career and to his own future in banking? No wonder he was so upset at the disappearance of his bodyguard, who must have accompanied him in his indiscretions! Everything's beginning to fall into place now. Remember what Memo's grandmother said about the young man's violent temper? Hernandez was on drugs. That also explains why he never had enough money."

"Which still leaves us," I reminded, "with two unsolved kidnappings."

"Yes, it does," Weston conceded. "And we're mighty short of leads. I suppose we'll have to go inside and ask a few questions."

"But they might be the kid—"

"That's neither here nor there. Honestly, John, sometimes you're too timid. Be bold."

Geoff stepped forward from the shadows and began whistling as he strode good-naturedly through a barrage of clothing toward apartment C. I followed, smiling stiffly by muttering "cheese." My partner sauntered up to the door and rapped it sharply with his knuckles.

"Let us in. Me enviaron Alma e Irma."

"Just a cotton pickin' minute," growled a male voice. I could hear sandals slapping toward us. Finally the door eased open a few inches and a suspicious eye examined us.

"Alma and Irma who? How come I never seen you before?"

"Actually," I admitted, "we're friends of Salvador Guerrero."

"Never heard of 'im."

The door began to close but Geoff inserted a foot.

"Maybe," my partner prompted pleasantly, "you know him by a different name. He's in his mid-twenties, slender, proud, has a thin nose—"

"Oh, him. I guess you're all right. Come on in and join the fun," offered the bushy-faced fellow, swinging the door open.

As we crossed the threshold, I had my first glimpse of "fun." Blankets lay rumpled here and there. Orange crates served as the only furniture. And emaciated occupants sat on the floor with their backs propped up against whatever wall was handy. The honey-sweet smell of marijuana hung heavy in the air. A pimply young "Prince Valiant" puffed on a butt and whispered slurringly into his girlfriend's ear. His girlfriend or pet—I wasn't quite sure which—had a dog collar around her scrawny neck and he held the other end of the leash.

"We are here," Weston informed the shaggy doorman (apparently the leader), "because our friend has disappeared under suspicious circumstances and . . . "

The pet in the corner giggled uncontrollably and snatched the butt. Mucus from her runny nose dribbled over her upper lip as she sucked deeply, sniffed and burst into more mindless giggles.

" . . . and we're trying to locate him."

Our host scowled and spat on the floor.

"You don't look like pigs," he decided, "and neither of you's his old man. What's it to you?"

A Latin-looking girl in a short blouse and hip-hugger jeans—setting off a painted belly button—put her arms around him, stroking his waist-length tresses.

"Come on, honey," her husky voice beckoned. "I need some Lucy in the Sky with Diamonds. Let's go fly together."

Shaggy pushed her away gently.

"Not now, Moonstone. Can't you see Papa's busy. Sit down and wait your ticket."

She obediently squatted, and looked at us sharply through bloodshot eyes.

"Well, man, what's your game? Out with it. We ain't got all day."

"That last statement," Weston responded grimly, "is at least true. You may not have much time left at all. For your information we're here because we actually care about other human beings instead of simply using them. As Christians we—"

"WOO WOO WOO WOO." The hooting spread around the room and became deafening as it was picked up by everyone except one nodding buck who seemed content to support his chin with his chest. "WOO WOO WOO." A baby on one of the blankets awoke and started crying. Moonstone jumped up and began squealing and bouncing about like a cheerleader. My jaw hung limply as I watched the display.

Out of the corner of my eye I noticed a black man get to his feet and slip over and stand in front of the door. Our way of escape was cut off. I began praying as I'd never prayed before. Shaggy raised his arms. and the hooting died quickly away. But every eye was nailed to us.

"Crud!" he growled. "A couple of Jesus freaks. I thought we'd seen the last of you at the border."

"Let's have a freak show," an empty-eyed giggler managed to get out. "Preach! Preach!" I could see needle marks on her bare arms.

The cry was taken up by the laughing, coughing inmates but faltered when Shaggy continued glaring at us.

"Why can't you filthy meddlers let brothers and sisters do their own thing in peace instead of giving us a hard time? 'Repent. Be saved.' We've heard it all! So why babble on like a stuck record?"

"Do you really want to know?" Weston demanded. "Or do you just want to give your 'groupies' more reason to act like animals?"

Silence fell like a rock. The black man's hand slid into his pocket. Both anger and respect flickered across Shaggy's face.

"I'll say this for you," he chuckled. "You've got guts. Yeah, I really want to know. Lay it on me."

"We talk to you," Geoff obliged, "because that's *our* thing. We're committed to love. And by that I don't mean some amorphic mushy slogan or sex 'trip.' We love Jesus *and* you, and He commanded us to tell you . . . so we do. If you've got any complaints, you'd jolly well better take them up with Him."

"But you," our host sneered, "are so much more convenient." He pulled a switchblade knife from his pocket; it clicked open. "And, of course, we wouldn't want to stop you from doing your thing. Sister over there," he said, pointing with the blade to a fourteen-year-old by the window, "really digs getting strung out on weed. And God made it. Tell me, is she going to fry and fry in *hell*?"

Sister and the rest of the group tittered—thoroughly enjoying the sport.

"Before I answer that," Geoff smiled, "let me correct a misstatement. In one sense God didn't make marijuana.

You did. There wasn't any in the Garden of Eden."

For the first time Shaggy showed a glimmer of interest. "Wha-a? You mean if I stepped into a time machine and went on back . . ."

"You wouldn't find Acapulco gold," Weston repeated. "Thorns and *weeds* came up when God cursed us for being ungrateful rebels. The weed in every reefer in this room is a reminder of that. Yet you smoke it."

"Yeah!" Moonstone grabbed the butt from Pet and stuck it in her mouth. "Look everybody, I'm smoking a curse. Ha ha. I'm—"

"Can it!" Shaggy snapped. "Buddy, there are lots of good things made from weeds—from rope to medicine."

"Indeed there are," my partner agreed. "God put mercy even in the curse. But everything in this world has designed functions. And to ignore them is sheer lunacy. It makes as much sense to dine on rock sandwiches and mercury tea as it does to bake your brains with hallucinogens, speed, and weed. You have a designed function too, you know."

"Maybe," the black man behind us drawled, "our purpose is to get high—as high as a birdie in the sky."

"Your purpose," Weston shot back, "is to first of all remain what God made you—someone created in His own image. God, my friend, isn't some irrational 'pot head.' If He were, He would have created a universe so crazy you'd all fall upward into space and explode like firecrackers. God is intelligent, rational, and caring. You should be, too. Your second reason for living is to serve Him. And you can only do that if you—yes, I'll use the words—'repent' of your sin, recognize Christ as the one who paid the debt on the cross, and are 'saved' by surrendering to Him in simple faith."

"And then," Pet sassed with a mocking grin, "I'll have Holy Ghost highs and be sucked into the clouds and spin around and around and—"

"Nothing of the sort," I interrupted. "You'll have self-control. That's the last of the Holy Spirit's fruits in a life—along with love, joy, peace, and a few others."

"You'll even," Geoff added, "be able to live with yourself rather than having to avoid lucid moments."

Pet ran her fingers playfully along her chain. "Aw, please don't say that, mister." She giggled at some hilarious secret joke. "I only get stoned on pot. "It's . . . it's not like I was a dope fiend or something. I mean, you probably smoke cigarettes or drink a little."

Weston stared shrewdly at her. "I'm sorry to disappoint you, but I don't. And, young lady, you're a liar. You use far more than marijuana. But if you want the argument answered, I'll be happy to."

She lit up another "reefer" and stuck it in her lips. "If you think you can, freak. I'm sitting in front of your monkey cage."

"And I'm standing in front of your rib cage," Geoff retaliated. "You're a walking skeleton. But personalities aside, write me a list of every drug you've ever taken."

"Why should I do that?"

Weston's voice softened almost to a whisper, and he leaned forward.

"You can't, can you? Because you don't know. Thousands of years ago Lot's daughters got him 'stoned' and seduced him. He didn't even remember what had happened. And you're just like him. Who knows what you've swallowed or injected during those marijuana highs? You don't."

Panic flashed in her eyes. "But my friends, they wouldn't—"

"Wouldn't know what they were giving you?"

Shaggy stepped quickly between Weston and the girl. His face was contorted with rage.

"Cut the bull, man. You're scaring one of my chicks. Everybody knows all the great mystics, including Jesus, turned on. That's how they had their visions. So stop with your con job."

"Jesus," my partner answered coldly, "wouldn't even let himself be doped when He had spikes driven through His hands and two-inch thorns stuck in His brow. He was 'clean'—totally clean. A lamb without spot or blemish who underwent agony for us. You, on the other hand, sir, are a spineless vegetable trying to escape from the imperfect world you helped produce, taking pot shots at God along the way in order to rationalize your own flight into irrationality."

Shaggy took a deep breath and the room exploded with his piercing animal yell. His body quivered as he flashed the point of the knife wildly in front of Geoff's face.

"Nobody! Nobody says that to me and lives! You stinking Christian! You're gonna go to that 'heaven' you like so much. You're flesh is gonna rot right here on this floor! It'll feel real good carving you up like a Christmas turkey!"

My partner forced himself not to look as the blade whipped under his chin. He blinked, but that was all. "Are you sure?" he replied icily.

"Am I sure *what*?" Shaggy hissed.

"That it will 'feel real good.' You feel with the mind, you know. And you've thrown a monkey wrench in there. Maybe you'll just think you feel real good. Maybe I'm not even here. Maybe I'm you and when I die you will too. Maybe you, old chap, are on a trip and I'm one of your chicks. Maybe I'm on a trip and you don't even exist and just think you do. Perhaps we're all just a three-dimensional-mirage projected into a bowl of jello. Perhaps . . ."

"Stop!" Shaggy put his hands to his forehead. "Aren't you real? You feel real. I mean . . ."

"Isn't it odd," Geoff suggested, "that Jesus freaks are always following you around? Did God send me? Or was it that tiny spark of sanity still left somewhere near your core that called me? Am I heightened consciousness or the aberration of a shattered mind?"

Weston turned his back on the leader and began walking toward the door.

"Excuse me, soul brother. You're in my way if I am, and you are, and the way is. Please move over." The black man dazedly stepped aside. "Thank you. And if any of you want to visit, knock on the door to the National Palace . . . if you have arms."

Weston swept through the door and out into the courtyard as hippies stood transfixed and confused. In utter amazement I followed.

"The same goes for me," I declared as firmly over my shoulder as I could. "Just think of me as the hallucination's hallucination."

Once outside I ran frantically—ducking under clotheslines, slapping aside damp sheets, and praising the Lord with every stride for our deliverance. Weston was only a step ahead and extending himself to his limits. I knew his goal—

to disappear into the tunnel before the hippies looked into the courtyard—and I was in complete agreement. As we neared the corner, I grabbed a protruding pipe and catapulted into the passageway, Geoff scooped up our bundle of belongings, and we half-skated through the slimy tunnel to the entrance. I was never so happy to see a bustling city street in my life! We ran along the sidewalk against traffic and waved wildly to our approaching cabbie. Even before the taxi came to a stop, we swung open the door and jumped in. There was no need for instructions. The driver floored the accelerator and we rushed away as if fleeing the devil himself.

Chapter 5

Diamonds, a Pyramid, and a Triangle

The lift operator closed the cage and we started creakily upward. Stairs spiraled around us and we passed several people descending on foot. The outer wall beyond the stairs was glass—etched with beautiful flowers now rendered almost invisible by urban grime. We were back in the now familiar and welcome confines of the palace. As a further reminder of our location, the bodyguard that had left us moments ago at the front gate had returned to his role as a soldierly mother hen.

"When you come right down to it," I mused out loud, "our boldness did not produce all that much information. From what we saw and heard, we pretty well know the kinds of drugs Salvador was subjected to. But as far as clues to his whereabouts or to friends who might have accompanied him on his escapades, we came up empty."

"It didn't seem appropriate," Weston quipped, "to ask those kinds of questions. There are two things of which I'm certain from our visit, however. The listening device isn't connected with the hippies. They could neither have gotten in to plant it nor have saved up enough money after 'highs' to afford it."

"They could," I disagreed, "have stolen the equipment."

Geoff extracted a bag of peanuts from his pocket and absent-mindedly tore the cellophane. "Yes, I suppose so. But they didn't strike me as very adept burglars. What's more, the receiver wasn't in their room. The second thing we've learned is that the listening device is either being monitored by a recorder, has been abandoned, or isn't being acted upon. If the owners actually heard our conversation in Salvador's room, they may suspect a police trap. Or they may already have what they want—namely the President's son. In either case, they didn't show any eagerness to close in on the commune."

"Wise chaps," I remarked ruefully. "But it wouldn't hurt to put Héroes de Nacozari under surveillance just in case. It's even possible, you know, that our bearded friends watched Salvador overdose and die on the premises. Addicts have been known to sneak out at night for a fix."

Geoff upended the peanut packet into his mouth. "Old boy, there's still the problem of secrecy. I'm afraid surveillance is out. But I wouldn't worry too much that our client is buried under a clothesline pole. If he is, so is Memo. And two drug deaths in the same week is more coincidence than I care to swallow. Even if the bug was planted by some splinter party rather than by kidnappers, I doubt the commune is involved in the disappearance."

"Who's talking about coincidence," I objected. "Shaggy may have gotten hold of a bad batch of dope."

The lift groaned to a stop at the third floor. We thanked the operator in Spanish, stepped out, and began our stroll along walkway balconies toward our quarters a couple of courtyards away. The military policeman followed the entire distance—keeping a careful three steps behind.

As we approached our rooms, I felt for our key. But it wasn't necessary. The door stood wide open and a bevy of uniformed policemen were in the process of disassembling everything from easy chairs to lighting fixtures. Screwdrivers, knives, and crowbars twisted, slit, poked and pried unmercifully. The President had relayed our request to Porfirio. The Inspector, in fact, was seated at our folding table—now moved to the center of the living room. Seemingly oblivious to the confusion, he was browsing through a stack of newspapers while a young lady with liquid brown eyes looked over his shoulder. Judging from her fine features and sharp chin, I guessed she was Salvador's sister.

"Well," Weston greeted jovially as we breezed in, "what have we here? The Inspector reading a scandal sheet like ¡Alarma! I'm surprised at you, Robledo. And here I thought you were a man of culture."

Porfirio dropped the periodical on the table and smiled.

"Not only *¡Alarma!*, Señor. I have also developed a taste for *Excelsior, Novedades, Avance, Oposición* and a few others. The ransom note has arrived, and the kidnappers seem to favor those publications."

"May we see the letter?"

"¿Cómo no? Of course. But be careful. The words are pasted on with flour glue that does not stick very well."

"I take it," I remarked as he held it out to us, "that you've tested for fingerprints."

"With no results. The envelope tells us nothing either— except that the letter was mailed yesterday."

"Now that," Weston exclaimed, "is cockiness! They sent off their demands before they'd even perpetuated the crime! Let's see if we can take the rascals down a peg or two."

He held the note so both of us could get a good look at it, and we translated to ourselves as we read.

> "We have your son. If you want him back alive, put one hundred million pesos worth of flawless, standard cut diamonds weighing less than one carat each in a brown leather pouch. Have Taylor put it at eight o'clock tomorrow morning on top of the Pyramid of the Sun. Don't mark the bag or contents with chemicals or Salvador dies. We will scan radio frequencies. If transmitter is in bag, it will be too bad! If you doubt that, look in the little pond by Chapultepec Castle. We are serious! This is the first and last letter. Don't stall."

"Why," I exclaimed, "that's incredible! They knew about us almost before we'd arrived here."

"And more importantly," Geoff reflected, "they wanted us to know they knew. They don't mind if we suspect an inside job, and they want to impress us with the need to comply exactly with their wishes. They could have gotten the information, of course, from the bug in Salvador's apartment."

"Two," Porfirio corrected. "We found another in a living room lamp."

The young lady behind the Inspector cleared her throat to attract attention.

"Mr. Weston, I've been waiting to speak with you because my father said you had some questions. If you can spare a moment to do that, then I'll leave you alone to conduct police business and get poor Salvador back."

My partner appraised our guest with a measure of respect. She was dressed simply in tan slacks and an open-throated print blouse. Her hair was her only jewelry—long, black, and brushed to a soft shine. And her deep voice betrayed the same direct, no-nonsense attitude.

"I will be most happy to, Miss Guerrero," Geoff assured her. "Could you start by telling me your first name? It's awfully awkward to address one another as Miss and Mister. I'm Geoff."

Her perfect teeth gleamed as she smiled. "And I'm Paloma. You must help my brother. Things look blacker every hour, don't they?"

"Not at all," Weston disagreed. "The most vulnerable time for kidnappers is that moment when they pick up the ransom. And now that a demand has been made, our chances for success have improved markedly. What I am concerned about, however, is Memo's fate. I have a feeling he'll be in that lake."

"But that's horrible!"

"Yes, it is," Weston frowned. "Murder is an insult to God and the human race. I believe, however, we'll both track down the killers and rescue Salvador."

Paloma nodded her head seriously.

"I will be praying for that, Mr. . . . Geoff. The worst part about all of this is that my brother is not prepared to die. It's funny, isn't it? With a name like Salvador he has no savior. I have been talking to him ever since I gave my heart to Jesus, but he says religion is only for women and old men."

"Perhaps," I suggested, "he'll remember your words now that he's in danger. Let's hope so."

"I take it," Weston probed, "that your brother didn't confide in you concerning his leisure-time activities."

Paloma's hands tightened on the back of the Inspector's chair.

"No, he didn't. I know he sometimes stayed out very late, though. He became furious with me once for asking him about it."

"To your knowledge," Geoff pursued the train of thought, "did anyone besides Memo ever accompany him?"

"Only Maria. Up until a month ago she was his novia—his fiancée."

"Could you give me a complete name and address?" he asked, trying to mask his surprise concerning this new development.

"Certainly. It is Maria de Jesus Ayala, and she lives in a quaint little Japanese house on Paseo de la Reforma. It's a couple of blocks south of the United States Embassy. I'm sorry I can't be more exact, but the building is one of a kind. I don't think you'll have difficulty finding it."

"I'm sure we won't," my partner beamed. "Is there anything else you know about Salvador or the kidnapping that you think would be of help to us? Anything at all?"

The girl studied the floor as she considered.

"Only that my brother is a very ethical and stubborn person. If the criminals holding him demand that he pose for a picture or call to ask the ransom be paid, he will not do it. You mustn't demand proof that he's alive. Other than that I can think of nothing. Tú sabes todo."

"Thank you," Geoff responded. "Rest assured that we will take your warning seriously. And we too will be praying. I'm sorry to have inconvenienced you. You're free to go." He shook her hand warmly. "If you think of anything else, feel free to get in touch."

"Don't worry," she promised solemnly, "I will."

As she moved gracefully toward the door, Porfirio shook his head in disbelief.

"You're an amazing man, Weston. You've known the President's daughter for four minutes, and already she's referring to you as 'tú.' I wasn't aware you had so much social grace."

"I have unmerited grace," Geoff corrected with a smile. "And that makes all the difference. Evangelicals view each other as members of the same family, so we use the familiar form for 'you.' That's all."

"Oh," the Inspector countered with an impish grin, "but I think it is more than that, my friend. Watch out or that woman will be wearing flowers in her hair for you."

I was about to come to Geoff's rescue when I noticed his

face reddening into a hot blush. And I wondered whether
. . . Porfirio saw the reaction, too, and burst into an exuber-
ant laugh. His stomach shook until he held it in pain.

"O qué . . . O qué, Weston! I never thought I would live
to see . . . You are human after all! When I read your 'report' in Paul's letter, I wondered. But there are a few old
things that have not been made new, aren't there?"

Several of the men in blue uniforms gazed with curiosity
at their boss, then went back to work. I could see that my
partner had the sincerest wish to dig himself a hole and
crawl in. And I must admit I was struggling to suppress my
own snickering.

"Your interpretation of those verses," I finally managed,
"leaves a bit to be desired, old chap. A more literal translation would be 'If any man is in Christ he's a new creation.
Those old things—judgments according to physical appearance alone—have passed by. Behold, new things have
come.' Paul was talking about the addition of a spiritual
dimension to life. Not about people being turned into heavenly robots."

"I can see," Porfirio ribbed good-naturedly, "that although physical appraisals have walked by, they sometimes
come back and tap one on the shoulder. Of course, in four
whole minutes maybe he has seen some," his eyes twinkled,
"great spiritual qualities in her, no?"

Unable to control myself any longer, we both convulsed
with laughter, filling the room with our roaring until we
were unsure if we could ever stop. Geoff even began chuck-
ling at himself. The policemen politely smiled, and
shrugged their shoulders, staring at us, then each other, in
puzzlement.

"I'll admit it," Weston confided as he fought for control,
"she's a pretty girl. But . . . But let's get a grip on ourselves.
Good grief! We're here investigating a serious crime. What
must people be thinking."

"But then," Robledo gasped, "they are judging from
. . . No, I will not say it. Oh, amigos, you are the best kind of
friends a man could have! You know how to laugh."

"Oh, brother, do we," I agreed. "But Geoff's right.
There's a lot of work ahead."

The Inspector took a deep breath and held it until his
face turned even redder, then exhaled slowly.

"There." He folded his hands in front of him. "Now, gentlemen, what do you suggest we do about the payoff? It will be very difficult to bring together that many real gems in time."

"On the other hand," I pointed out, "if they're asking payment in untraceable stones, they must know the ins and outs of the jewelry business. They may even have a jeweler in the gang. To throw in counterfeits would be extremely dangerous."

"I have to agree with John," Weston observed. "But before we go any further, would you please make sure the search for bugs is complete enough so we can be confident we're not Mexico City's newest radio attraction?"

The Inspector slapped his forehead in consternation. "Of course. How careless of me." He hailed a policeman who was passing by carrying a curtain rod. "¿Teodoro, cómo va la investigación? Is it safe to speak?"

"Just so long," the sergeant warned laconically, "as you don't tell any more jokes. People have died from milder convulsions. Seriously, Inspector, there's nothing to worry about. We're starting to put the room back together."

"Thank you," Porfirio nodded affably, "for both the advice and the information. You may carry on with your duties."

"As I was about to say," Weston resumed the conversation, "we had better comply with the kidnappers' demands precisely. From their use of language, they appear to be well schooled. They certainly have money enough to purchase the radio monitoring equipment they claim to have. And a search of that pond will almost surely prove their ruthlessness. At the same time, of course, we'll be risking millions of pesos."

"And how do you propose," Porfirio inquired, "that we minimize that risk without endangering the hostage?"

"If I'm to put the ransom on top of a pyramid," I ventured, "then they're obviously planning to pick it up from the air. The blighters might be tracked by helicopter at a safe distance—provided our radar is more sophisticated than theirs."

"A good idea," the Inspector agreed. "Geoff, have you anything to add?"

My partner pulled on his goatee in his characteristic

manner. "Only," he reflected, "that ground-based heat and sound-sensing devices might add some insurance. If you would equip a jeep for us, I'd appreciate it."

Robledo nodded. "Done. Is there anything else?"

"Yes, there is," Geoff admitted. "But I don't know how you or the President will take to the suggestion. The North Americans have a spy satellite that could monitor every square inch for miles around the pyramid. I'd like the Mexican government to ask for its use."

Creases showed on the Inspector's forehead.

"That, of course, I cannot guarantee. From a purely investigatory standpoint it would, no doubt, be a breakthrough—if the Americans cooperate. But then, it might also cause some to ridicule our police force as inadequate. And there are those in the government who are not that friendly with the Americans. We are a sovereign nation, and a show of dependence like that . . . Well, you understand."

"I am well aware of the political implications," Geoff pressed. "But I also know that it's the only foolproof way to track the diamonds. The kidnappers could drop the sack from a helicopter or glider onto the deck of a truck and radar would be useless. At least bring the matter up with Guerrero."

Porfirio rose to his feet.

"That much at least I promise. But if other Latin American countries found out we were using a spy satellite . . . Well, I have much to do between convincing the President, equipping the jeep, dragging the pond, and helping to collect diamonds. I'd better get started. Oh, before I forget, here's your knife." He took it from his pocket and slid it across the table.

"Many thanks," Weston responded as he picked it up. "We'd best be running too. But we'll have our motorcar back here in plenty of time to be fitted. You may also bump into us at the lake. Cheerio."

* * * * *

The clattering of the VW engine was not at all reassuring to someone accustomed to driving a Mercedes. But the jeep seemed dependable enough. And it was perfect for maneuvering in the inner city. Paseo de la Reforma spread before us with multiple lanes, islands, and a traffic circle every few blocks. It was a gorgeous street—the showcase of the city. Tall trees lined the sidewalks. Curbside statues stood guard. And monuments commemorating the nation's history jutted above almost every circle. Cuauhtémoc the Indian stared sternly down at us. Winged liberty flew majestically atop her marble pillar. And, almost as impressive, one single pedestal was missing—replaced by a yellow rose garden. Somebody had fallen into disfavor.

We passed vintage office buildings and flashy skyscrapers of pancaked cement and glass. Full-grown coconut palms even sprouted from one roof. The massive United States Embassy slipped by on our right, with its heavy fence and mace-spike decorations between floors. No wonder, I reflected, the Yanks had an image problem here. They could have used far gentler architecture! As I slowed to change lanes, a middle-aged gentleman in an electric green suit and feathered hat passed me on, of all things, a mini-bike! He toted a briefcase and his knees and elbows were flung out into the breeze. Talk about image! I swung our vehicle into the right lane since we were nearing Miss Ayala's house.

"That must be it," Geoff pointed appreciatively. "Look, there's a parking space right out front. Have you got change for the meter?"

"That depends," I informed him, "on whether it takes small, medium or large veintes. These people change their coin sizes so often it's amazing vending machine operators don't all go bald pulling their hair out."

"Well," Weston responded, "see if you can jam something in. Better that than the police garage!"

I stopped the motorcar and, although unaccustomed to a steering wheel on the left, backed into the space with remarkable ease. The meter took the newer veintes, and I had a supply. We whistled optimistically as we approached the ivy-covered fence, and I punched the buzzer.

On the other side of the barrier, an Oriental brownstone sat like some diminutive castle on the lawn. Its three ski-slope roofs rose to tiled points, and the high center tower resembled a belfry honeycombed with archways. One wing sported a vaguely Dutch-gabled bonnet above windows that peeked out at us sleepily through half-closed lids.

"Now that," Weston enthused, "*is* a unique building.

For. Lochead

It's petite, homey, and solid all at the same time."

"And," I agreed, "it's graceful. I don't believe I've ever seen a two-, five-, three-story house before. I like imagination."

"And I," Geoff echoed, "like promptness. Only fifteen seconds and the door's already opening. You'd think we'd fired a starter pistol!"

A young woman in a "granny" dress came running down the walk toward us. Her stringy blond hair streamed down over her shoulders and she clutched an armload of books with the desperation of a student about to be late for class. Before reaching the fence, however, she slowed to regain some dignity.

"Oh," she stammered, "Desculpen-me, por favor. I thought you were the taxi. You see I'd called them and—"

"We quite understand," I assured her. "I'm John Taylor and this is my partner, Geoffrey Weston. I take it that you're Maria de Jesus."

She nodded and unlatched the gate for us.

"We are here," Geoff took over, "investigating the kidnapping of Salvador Guerrero. I understand you and he—"

"Salvador kidnapped!" Her pouty lips opened in what seemed to be genuine astonishment. "But he can't be. Who would—"

"That," Weston broke in, "is precisely what we're trying to find out. I understand that you have accompanied him to some rather unsavory places—in fact, to drug parties. Perhaps you could tell us of one or two greedy revelers."

Her gaze faltered and for a moment she looked like a shy French girl; but then the Latin fire flashed. "Someone," she declared indignantly, "has told you a vicious lie, Mr. Weston. I've never gone to any such place. But I'll certainly answer any questions that might be of help."

"Oh, come now," my partner smiled. "You can be open with us. We're private detectives—not the police. Whatever you say will be used with discretion."

"It's not that," she insisted. "I tell you, you're simply wrong. I go to university plays and—"

"Miss Ayala," Weston interrupted sternly. "All we have to do is have the police interrogate the chaps on Nacozari Street to find out if you're telling the truth. But that might prove a trifle messy for both you and Salvador, don't you think?"

Maria blinked and threw her head back as if she'd been physically struck.

"Oh." Her voice broke. "So you know about that. It's not fair!"

"What," I inquired gently, "isn't fair? As reprehensible as your actions were, there'll be no arrest."

"Can't you see?" Maria's words tumbled end over end. "It's not you I'm talking about. Maybe you won't say anything. But sooner or later there'll be somebody else. It's society that isn't fair. People walk on their knees for blocks to the shrine of the Virgin of Guadalupe, and their friends congratulate them for bleeding all over the sidewalk. But if I, like Castañeda, try to approach God by taking drugs and having visions, then I'm an outlaw. I have to sneek around in shadows and live in fear that someday someone like you will come to my door and point his finger at me!"

Geoff frowned as he scrutinized the girl. "Perhaps," he countered, "*neither* you nor what you call 'society' is being fair to God."

"What do you mean?"

"Simply that both of you seem to picture Him as some illogical, capricious tyrant. If you would definitely commit yourself to the idea that the Lord is practical, your spiritual search would be over."

"I'm afraid," she admitted, "that you're being too cryptic for me."

Weston took a deep breath and gestured with his hand. "All right, then, let me put it this way. Is God all-knowing and present everywhere?"

"Why, of course." She managed a weak smile. "This is beginning to sound like catechism class."

"And," Geoff continued, "is the Lord all knowing *because* He's everywhere?"

"That," she decided, "would stand to reason. It would be easiest for Him to know what was happening if He were around."

"Then, don't you think the most effective way to communicate with God would be to simply talk to Him?"

"But we must pray to the blessed Virgin," she said earnestly. Her face showed her confusion. "Mary doesn't have those properties, I suppose, or she'd be God, but we've been instructed to . . . "

"Now," countered Geoff, "you're defending the very system you criticized a moment ago. Consider, though, what takes place if one *could* pray to Mary. If I pray to God, I have assurance in His very nature that He hears me. He's right in the room. But if I pray to Mary, either at home or at a shrine, how does she hear? Remember that thousands, perhaps millions, are talking to her at that very same time."

"I've never thought of that," Maria admitted thoughtfully. "I suppose God must pass on the messages to her."

My partner nodded. "That would seem to be the only logical way, wouldn't it—if the system is to be maintained. But this brings us to another problem. What does Mary do with the prayers once she has them?"

Miss Ayala stared past us as though trying to picture the answer in her catechism. "Mary," she ventured, "is the mother of God—that is, of Jesus. So she is able to influence Him to help us."

"Very interesting, indeed!" Geoff fairly beamed with satisfaction. "Now let's put these concepts together. First, we come up with a God who doesn't really love us enough to help. He has to be talked into it by his mother. Secondly, we have a God who loves His mother so little that He saddles her with the daily task of routing millions of prayers to Him—giving her virtually no time to enjoy heaven. Thirdly, we end up with an impractical God who chooses to maintain a system so cumbersome and involved, it would make even a bureaucrat blush. You pray to Mary. God hears you. Then God tells Mary what you told Mary so Mary can tell God what He told her you told Him to tell her to tell Him! In addition, you may have to convince her to take your case in the first place by crawling on bloody knees! Such a system is ridiculous. And its excesses all result from an imperfect view of God.

"However, your own attempt to reach God through drugs suffers from a similar flaw. You think that you must use drugs—physical substances which distort thought process—in order to communicate with a God who is spirit, and absolutely rational. You thus exercise a tremendous contradiction."

"I have never heard God explained to me in quite that

way," she conceded, as she shifted her books to her other arm and flexed numb fingers. "I will definitely think about what you have said. But I don't promise to turn into some 'straight.'"

"Just remember," my partner warned, "the next time you chew peyote or swallow LSD, I may be asking the Lord to give you a 'bad trip.'"

With fear and contempt in her voice she challenged, "You hardly know me. Besides, your job is to rescue Salvador from kidnappers, not me from a few drugs. Why all this fatherly concern?"

"Because," I interjected, "you need to stop using drugs before they do permanent damage to you."

"And," Geoff added in a soft but firm tone, "because your actions are an affront to God. You picture yourself, I take it, as a second Carlos Castañeda being instructed by some counterpart to the Indian witch doctor don Juan. Is that correct?"

"Yes, it is. But I don't see—"

"Precisely. You don't see. If you did, you'd run in terror from what you've been attempting." Weston held up a finger. "Remember this one point. God is practical, logical, and loving. But the god recorded in Castañeda's journal doesn't seem to me to be any of these three. What was don Juan's message to Carlos? Simply that there are no gifts. . . . Everything has to be worked for.

"And what was Castañeda's first supernatural sensation while he was working for the right to get 'high' on peyote? He was sent into a panic by some force that took control of his body and caused his hands to bend into the shape of claws. Miss Ayala, Carlos had a brush with a demon.

"A loving God doesn't establish drugs as a road to knowing Him," Weston affirmed, "since He'd be responsible for every O.D. and human vegetable by the wayside. A practical God doesn't either, since He'd be favoring those healthy enough to sustain drugs, and able to afford them. And a logical God would hardly depend on pills that squeeze the very juice of logic out of a man. The god you've attempted to contact is one that cackles in the night and destroys human lives for a thrill. You've been trying to commune with Satan."

A gentle breeze brushed through Maria's hair as she stared silently at us, motionless. Finally I felt I had to say something to fill the void.

"Miss Ayala," I urged, "there *is* a gift. Jesus bought eternal life for you when He died and made complete payment for your sins—even your sin of worshipping the devil. If you surrender your life and heart to Him, He'll give that life to you. Then you'll have what you've been searching for."

A solitary tear wandered down her cheek. "I still do not understand how you could be so concerned about me as . . . I see a taxi coming. Are there any questions about Salvador that . . . "

"Yes," Geoff inquired, "were any others at the parties besides the hippies, you, your novio, and Memo?"

"No. It would have been too risky."

"What about Salvador's health? Was it good?"

"I guess . . . " Maria shrugged. "A little drowsiness, some headaches and bad dreams—as you said, taking drugs has side effects."

A bright yellow motorcar slowed and double-parked in front of the house. The driver looked our way and honked impatiently.

"I'll have to go now, Mr. Weston." She backed toward the curb. "I hope I've been of help."

"One more question," Geoff insisted loudly. "Why did you break your engagement with Salvador?"

She turned and ran out into the street.

"I didn't," she called over her shoulder. "*He* broke it off. He had another girlfriend. I don't know who."

The door slammed and the taxicab sped away leaving us to ponder a new twist in the affair.

Maria Ayala's home was only a few minutes away from Chapultepec Forest, so we drove off to check on the investigation at the castle pond. Paseo de la Reforma continued in all its splendor, cutting a swath between banks, hotels, government buildings, and tourist snares. Only one snagged my senses: the red brick Flaminia Tea Salon with its large colonial windows and tempting exotic aromas. Our jeep snarled past a bronze Diana the Huntress standing naked in a fountain and lofting arrows at plate glass windows across the way.

In the "forest" proper, road signs eagerly invited us to visit the zoo, amusement park, and two or three different kinds of museums. Instead we skirted an exhibition hall of modern art and turned left toward Grasshopper Hill. Our map showed the woods were honeycombed with lakes, but there was one tiny one which seemed most likely.

The sidewalks were alive with children in red, green or yellow-checked school uniforms, and a chorus of vendors hawking peanuts, popcorn, balloons and trinkets. As the road curved, we could make out Maximilian's castle on the hill. There were so many pines on the slope, however, that we couldn't quite tell where the hill ended and the castle began.

I pointed to a cluster of parked motorcars down the street. "There they are, Geoff. And it looks like the police have come up with something."

"They have, indeed." Weston eyed the draped stretcher being wheeled to the curb. "What do you think the chances are that the poor blighter was somebody's bodyguard?"

I shook my head sadly as I brought the jeep to a stop behind the last police cruiser. "Too good," I sighed. "Perhaps he stumbled onto the plot to kidnap the President's son and was killed for his trouble."

Geoff pulled up the door handle. "That would explain the boast to his sister, wouldn't it? He could have been gathering evidence, expecting a reward. He might also have tried blackmailing the kidnappers."

Inspector Robledo was helping lift the stretcher into the coroner's ambulance, so we strolled toward him, passing an asphalt path which probably led down to the water.

Porfirio caught sight of us and vigorously flapped his arm. "Hurry up, amigos, if you want to view the body." He hesitated. "I think you will find it most interesting."

Geoff and I spurred ourselves to a trot. The ambulance driver was turning over the engine as we arrived. Porfirio gingerly pulled back the sheet. I was glad we hadn't stopped for tea and biscuits. The once-handsome young man was now white and slimy, with hideously puckered skin from remaining submerged. Manacles on his arms and legs told part of the story. He'd been weighted down so he wouldn't float. A flat spot on the back of his skull told the rest.

"You were correct," Porfirio recounted, "about his being hit from behind with a rock. We've detected traces of sandstone in the roof scratches. And I imagine the medical examiner will find more of the same. The poor devil never knew what hit him. If he had any secret information, one thing is certain. He died with it. You don't suppose Salvador was taken because they'd failed with Memo, do you?"

I almost chuckled in spite of the grisly sight lying before me. "Inspector," I pointed out, "one hundred million pesos in ransom hardly sounds like an afterthought."

"Yes," Robledo agreed reluctantly. "They must have been after your client all along." He draped the sheet back over the corpse and slammed the door ferociously. As the thud echoed off the hill, the ambulance eased away from the curb with, surprisingly, its siren wailing.

"We were negligent," Porfirio concluded, "in not suspecting a kidnap plot. But Salvador had a whole company of guards to protect him. I don't know what more we could have done."

"The abduction," Weston sympathized, "was unpreventable with the meager knowledge we had then. So stop feeling guilty, old fellow. Why don't we wander on down to the pond and you can fill us in on new developments."

My partner patted the Inspector on the back and steered him toward the curb.

"I would be happy to," our friend agreed. "But I'm afraid you already know everything we know. This is the most baffling case I've ever come up against. It's a puzzle within a puzzle within a puzzle, and there don't seem to be any answers. Only more questions."

"What about," I prompted, "your investigation of the palace roof? Surely—"

"It yielded nothing," Porfirio snapped. "There were no scratches. No indication whatsoever that anyone had crossed over from another building on ropes. Personally, I doubt that they did. There were soldiers stationed on every side of the building, so anyone attempting such a feat would have been shot down like a pigeon."

"Yet," I pursued, "people so seldom look up that the guards might have missed them."

"No," Robledo declared flatly, "that couldn't have happened. With a structure a block long and only three or four stories high, guards at the corners didn't even have to look above eye level to see the roof line a half block away. I tell you, the kidnappers could not have come across the roof."

Birds chirped merrily and there was rustling in the branches as we started down the path. Neatly clipped shrubs and spear-pointed succulents lined the asphalt. But after a few yards pines and pin oaks, firs and hackberries crowded out the sky. My spirit felt the calm of what seemed like a wilderness glen.

"I take it," Geoff observed, "that the sewers and the tube station didn't afford any way in. You would have mentioned it."

Porfirio broke off a leaf from one of the shrubs and chewed it absent-mindedly as we strolled. "Of course," he confirmed. "Nobody came in from underneath. I would be inclined to suspect an electric-powered hang glider if there were such a thing—which there isn't. A parachute might account for the entrance but not the escape. And the airport control tower reports no traffic over the palace that evening."

"Which leads us to the inescapable conclusion," Weston nodded cheerfully, "that the kidnappers were already inside when the gates closed for the night. All they had to do was elude the courtyard guards."

"And," I finished, "make an impossible escape disguised as soldiers carrying a drunken comrade."

"Except," Porfirio burst the bubble, "that everyone who left that night has been logged and accounted for. I still like the glider idea. A single man could have jettisoned his motor in a park a few blocks away, have landed on the roof, and later have glided off the roof to the courtyard in the square."

"Which," Geoff added skeptically, "was brightly lighted and within plain view of the guards. What's more, the wind was blowing the wrong way—I've already checked. I congratulate you, nonetheless, on your imagination. It's a rare ingredient these days and well worth nurturing."

"How do you propose then," Robledo countered with a tinge of exasperation, "that the dogs succeeded in their crime?"

At that moment we rounded a bend and came within

sight of the pond—a kidney-shaped widening of a narrow, stone-lined canal. A wooden footbridge crossed its throat at the end nearest us, and the path led directly to it.

"I have a notion," Weston confided, "but I'm afraid it's even wilder than yours. I think I'd better keep it under my hat until there's some evidence."

Several small children came running past us, panting and jabbering noisily. "I tell you I saw him. He looked like a zombie that . . . Mama says on the Day of the Dead . . . Wonder who killed him. I hope he's not hiding behind any bushes. . . . The murderer's gonna get you, Luci . . . "

We stepped up onto the bridge and gazed at the water. I couldn't tell how deep it was; thick algae had dyed the water an opaque green. The surface, though, was vivid with the reflection of evergreens and oaks. No wonder the corpse hadn't been discovered earlier.

Porfirio leaned out over the handrail and pointed. "When they dumped the body, it landed about there. It didn't seem they threw it—just rolled it over the railing."

"Which means," I interrupted, "that a single strong chap could have done the job. What about the gate back at the road? Was it kept locked? I assume they came at night."

"Indeed, they did. Someone broke the chain. But since the caretaker couldn't find any vandalism, he thought it was just a prank."

"I take it," Geoff remarked, "that you've thoroughly examined both the bridge and path . . . and also the mud at the bottom of the pond."

Porfirio pushed his glasses back into place.

"Yes, we have. And we didn't find anything. I'd hoped at least the murder weapon would be buried in the mire."

"Then," Weston concluded solemnly, "there's nothing more we can do here. Were you able to arrange for use of the satellite?"

The Inspector turned away and stepped back down onto the path. His shoulders drooped and for the first time I thought of him as old.

"Amigos," he mused. "This life is filled with compromises between quality and price. One does the best with what he has. The cost to our country's pride was just too high." He began retracing his steps toward the road. "El

Presidente would not hear of it."

On our way home my partner and I ventured into a small, unpretentious restaurant and sampled their specialty—steaming chile pie with a side order of enchiladas and goat meat tamales. Our trip to Mexico was worthwhile after all!

Back at the palace, we spent the rest of the afternoon helping install the sensing devices in our jeep and testing them out. Geoff also arranged to borrow a couple of regulation army pistols.

The evening was a relaxing one. We watched a rather absurd rerun of "La Mujer Bionica" on the tele and then settled down to some serious Bible study. We retired early, wondering what the morning would bring.

Chapter 6

The Wild Goose Chase

I gasped exorbitantly, but there just wasn't enough air. Finally at the second level, I sat down on a rough stone, panting. The plateau below looked like a flat rocky desert, punctuated occasionally by gnarled dwarf trees and circumscribed by low-lying mountains.

It was hard to conceive of myself being a mile and a half above sea level, but my lungs emphatically confirmed it. And I still had the two hardest levels to climb in order to reach the top of the pyramid!

Down below, six police cruisers and our jeep were scattered about like children's toys. I could barely distinguish the camouflage that covered the helicopter. The men had covered it meticulously, and from the top it appeared to be just another dry-land thicket. From the top! It was time to get moving again.

The kidnappers expected their money by eight, and I'd jolly well better not be late. I struggled to my feet and paused briefly to press my pounding temples. Why was it that every morning, now, I seemed to have a headache? Oh well, duty called. I thanked the Lord for the privilege of serving Him, and resumed climbing.

The stairway which had been extremely broad at the base, narrowed, and, to my dismay, the steps were now steeper and smaller. My heels protruded over the edge, so I finally resorted to leaning forward on my hands and almost crawling up the incline. I was careful not to knock loose the large leather pouch tied to my belt.

This, I thought to myself, is incredible! It was as if I were an ancient Aztec stumbling up to an altar to offer sacrifice

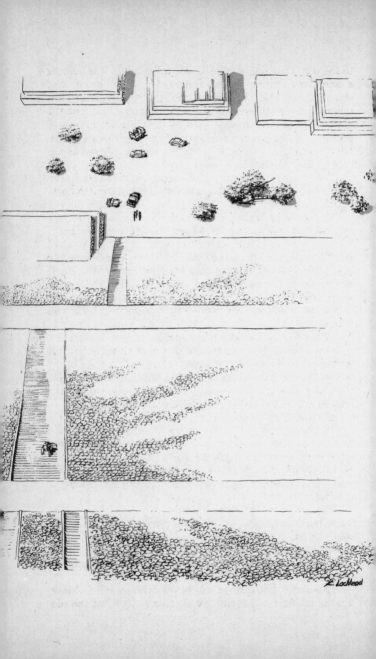

to the sun. I wondered whimsically if I actually was bearing a sacrifice. Perhaps some Indian separatist group had staged this whole thing as a political ploy. An airplane might fly over at any time and simply drop a bomb on the diamonds! Not at all comforted by the thought, I strained upward. My hands were irritated from the abrasive rock, but I forced them into a faster rhythm and clambered up the face of the "mountain."

The pyramid's summit was slightly rounded and altogether too small for my taste. I walked around a mite checking the surface for signs of tampering. There were none.

I looked toward the horizon and was struck by the majesty and silent emptiness of the land. There were no signs of humanity except for a nearby tourist museum and ancient ruins forming a path to the Pyramid of the Moon some two kilometers distant. I shook my head in sorrow. The futile monuments of a dead religion remained—slowly decaying while the builders screamed their eternal miseries—subjected to God's holy wrath. Idols had betrayed their worshippers.

I set the pouch down in the middle of the summit and gingerly approached the edge. Why was it always harder to get down off a roof than it was to climb it? In spite of my hurry, I began my descent in a sitting position like some toddler, in a slow bumpity-bump down the stairs. By the second level I was standing normally again and trotting.

My watch showed ten after eight. I didn't fancy still being on the rock face when our visitors showed up. Taking the last few steps two at a time, I puffed across clear ground and fairly collapsed onto the bonnet of our jeep.

"Bully for you, John!" Weston held out an apple cola for me. "You've established a new speed record for 'taking in' the pyramid!"

The Inspector drank deeply from his own bottle.

"Mas hay que decir," he added with a twinkle in his eyes, "that your performance lacked a little in grace and dignity. It's a good thing this whole affair is a secret, or you would have had some very uncomplimentary pictures in this afternoon's newspapers!"

"As well," I gasped painfully, "as several dozen blackguards trying to ventilate my skull and . . . steal the diamonds prematurely. I'm glad Guerrero stayed home."

Porfirio became serious. "You and I both. This payoff could have been a prelude to assassination." He laid his soda down, removed his glasses, raised binoculars to his eyes and searched the horizon. "Birds," he muttered. "Nothing but birds. Perhaps Eliseo is having better luck. They could be approaching from behind the pyramid."

Without comment, Geoff slid into the driver's seat and switched our newly installed radio to public address.

"Eliseo!" His voice echoed harshly across the desert. "What do you see from your angle?"

After a brief interval we heard someone blowing into a microphone.

"¡Nada! Nothing at all. ¡The sky is clear!"

Now somewhat recovered from my ordeal, I guzzled the carbonated apple juice and joined the vigil. Time seemed to slow and the minutes plodded lethargically. Sixteen of us stood at our appointed positions—waiting . . . watching . . . wondering. Porfirio was very ramrod and military and his gaze never faltered. He reminded me of Field Marshall Montgomery surveying the battlefield. Geoff was more relaxed—but every bit as intent. Nothing moved either on land or in the air except for that flock of birds heading south.

All at once Weston whirled about and aimed his binoculars almost straight up.

"Of course! A *brown* pouch. It had to be brown. It had to be leather. Shoot them down! All but the leader!" He drew his automatic and began firing rapidly into the air."

"Shoot who down?" Porfirio yelled. "There's nothing there. Get a grip on—"

"The birds!" Geoff outshouted him. "The birds! They're carrying pouches—except for one. Get the rifles from your motorcar before it's too late. John, order the others to fire." His pistol jumped in his hand again as he sent another volley skyward.

"¡Atención!" I screamed excitedly into the microphone. "¡Atención! Shoot down every bird carrying a pouch. I repeat, only those carrying pouches!"

I looked over at the cruiser and saw the Inspector fumbling frantically with his keys. There wouldn't be time. I drew my own pistol and pointed it skyward. I couldn't even jar a few feathers loose. I heard sporadic gunfire from one of the other observation posts, but it sounded like pistols too. Finally the high-pitched thwack of an automatic rifle pierced the air. But only two birds had fallen, and the others had already started to dive. I fired until the clip was empty. As I paused to reload, they disappeared over the rim of the pyramid.

Weston grabbed the mike and frantically ordered, "Stop firing! Stop firing! Don't shoot at the birds as they take off. There's no way of telling which has the diamonds. Get in your motorcars and prepare to give chase. Remove the camouflage from the helicopter. Break radio silence and decide among yourselves which birds you're going to follow. Then give it all you've got."

Porfirio, who had opened the cruiser's boot, slammed it closed and ran for the driver's door. I jumped into the back seat of the jeep, next to the tracking equipment. Geoff gunned the engine, and we were off. The birds were now circling overhead. As I gazed upward they began dividing off and heading in different directions.

"Which way are we going?" I shouted in Weston's ear. "Toward the city?"

"Not on your life, old chap. That route's too obvious." He switched the radio to a prearranged channel. "Inspector, do you hear me?"

"Sin duda, amigo," a voice crackled in answer. "Which bird do you want?"

"I'm taking the one heading northeast. Have fun with the rest."

"Very good. If you find the diamonds, don't forget to come back."

"Don't worry," Geoff responded. "Just make sure your men play by the same rules."

We vaulted over a ditch and flattened a tuna cactus as we howled through the desert, glutting the air with dust. I put on my earphones and worked furiously to aim the sound disk at the soaring bird. If I could just keep it lined up long enough to feed a noise pattern into the computer! That way we might be able to distinguish it later from background clutter, and whatever finches and starlings happened along. While I twisted the dials, I was jolted to the bone as we bucked and jerked across the terrain. We hurtled across a gully, mounted a knoll and careened down another rocky slope. The land had looked so flat from the pyramid, but it certainly didn't feel like it!

"What kind of bird is it?" I asked loudly. "And what are our chances?"

"It's a hunting falcon," Geoff shouted over the wind whistling past our ears. "And I'd say we have precious little chance! Any moment now I expect a tire to burst or that we'll crash into a ditch. Hold on and do your stuff! I'll try to maintain visual contact as long as I can!"

He swerved around a tree and we nearly tipped over when the right wheels slammed over rock. Weston downshifted. "I've got a fix on the bird!" I yelled. I set the dish for automatic tracking and concentrated on adjusting the heat sensor as a backup unit. But the task proved to be hopeless. With every third or fourth twist of a knob, the machine went wild from facing the sun.

"Hurry up and find a road," I challenged, "or we'll snap an axle!"

"We'll break our fool necks!" Weston shot back. "But there's nothing to be done about it. Political jealousy! That's the villain! We could be sitting back in easy chairs while the C.I.A. kept tabs on every pigeon in the pie. But no, Latin America wouldn't like that! If they thought for a minute, they'd realize that while the satellite was studying the migrating habits of the homing bird, it wouldn't be zeroing in on them. Watch out! Here comes a big one!"

We were airborn again—jumping a gully. And there were only a hundred more ahead of us. We both shut up and concentrated on keeping ourselves in one piece. My stomach began objecting to all the lurching and bouncing. Then the bugs began hitting—splattering on the windshield and flying over into our faces. The sound dish was a gooey mess in no time and I had to wipe it off continually and hope the computer could keep handling the signal overload. "Lord," I prayed, "lead us to a road!"

Several moments later the jeep scrambled up a bank onto a narrow ribbon of asphalt. And it seemed to parallel the direction of the falcon's flight—although it twisted, turned, and dipped more than the bird did. Geoff floored the accelerator; the speedometer needle went up to the top and stuck. Tires shrieked on every curve, but held—no doubt the cactus needles embedded in them added that extra margin of traction. My foot became weary from pushing an imaginary brake pedal, and more than once I closed my eyes, certain we would crash.

Now it wasn't just desert plants that flashed by. On every side stately pines obscured our vision, and it was nearly impossible to see our quarry. But we still had a sound fix.

Pine trees! I realized the horrible truth. We were nearing the eastern edge of the plateau where the rainfall was greater. Geoff and I were about to descend eight-thousand-foot mountains at breakneck speed! And there up ahead was a flat-bed lorry, rounding a bend in the road—on our side! Weston jammed the brakes and horn at the same time. The truck driver just barely got over.

A few kilometers farther along we had no trouble spotting the bird of prey. He was lazily riding the air currents over a mile-high canyon while we endeavored desperately to stick like mosquitos to cliff walls. The lucky blighter!

Again and again we had to pass slower motorists or avoid head-on collisions with trucks driving on the wrong side. We quickly learned that accepted driving technique entailed straightening the road out by steering over into the inside lane of every bend. My partner—an apt student—picked up the method with alarming ease.

Here and there we passed mangled guardrails where predecessors had gone over the edge. But most of the time there weren't even rails. Stick buildings with grass roofs offered colas, rocks, and 666 for sale. The latter—a linament—was supposed to be hot. I imagined so!

More and more often, we had to slow for naked toddlers playing by the road. Stick villages popped up. Larger cement towns took over wherever the land was flat enough and sometimes even when it wasn't. Cornfields began to checker the mountainsides. Coffee trees waved in the breeze. Spring water gushed and gurgled out of the cliff face by the side of the road. Lush undergrowth turned the world green. And the unrelenting falcon was pulling ahead of us as we squealed around bends and slammed on our brakes.

Hour after hour we plunged downward past donkey-drawn carts and yapping dogs, and the most breathtakingly beautiful scenery I had ever encountered. Then we lost the sound. Geoff slowed down to normal speed. It felt as if we were crawling. I searched manually. Nothing . . .

"Well," I shrugged, "we can always buy a parrot. There should be plenty of exotic birds around here if the twitter in the trees is any indication."

"He may have landed," Weston was trying hard to sound hopeful. "The next town is a place called Tamazunchale. We can ask around there."

I noticed a man up ahead, bent under an incredibly tall load of firewood. He was certainly carrying a hundred pounds on his back. His clothes were tattered. He needed a shave and his sandals had seen better days.

"There," I motioned, "is a fellow who's been around this neck of the woods for a while. Let's ask him."

"Why not."

We pulled off the road and stopped right in front of him.

"Excuse me," I shouted affably, "but we're looking for a chap who trains falcons. You wouldn't by chance know of anyone like that, would you?"

The peasant looked at us through ancient, sunken eyes.

"Sí, Señor. There is such a man. The old guitar maker in town. But he sold his last bird two months ago, maybe three. There is another man who has chachalacas and—"

"No," I interrupted. "We're only interested in falcons." I reached out the window and handed him a five-hundred peso bill and a gospel pamphlet I'd picked up in London. "Gracias!"

As we drove off he stared open-mouthed at his hand. I trust he was also impressed by the tract.

"So," Geoff reflected, "it's off to ye olde guitar shoppe. I'm beginning to smell a blind alley. You don't suppose, do you, that some slightly used merchandise has just been returned?"

We drove past a tropical motel and through the main residential district. An Indian mission and Presbyterian church clung to a hill to our right. Farther on we noted a motel, tire repair center, telegraph office, petrol station, and a bank. Men, women, and children walked about, enjoying leisurely conversations. I envied them.

My shirt was now wringing wet with perspiration; the lower altitude made quite a temperature difference. Cowboy hats were in vogue here. At the far end of town we neared a good-sized bridge spanning a crystal blue river. Orange trusses gave the bridge its structural strength. Judging from some mangled crossbars, they also served to shorten overly-tall lorries.

Just before the bridge, we turned left onto the town's main business street. It was barely two lanes wide and lined with one-story cement stalls. We rumbled past a dozen tiny shops . . . and there it was. Guitars hung from clotheslines, from ropes, from nearly everywhere—inside the store and out. There were also belts, whips, and other assorted leather goods. An old man in the doorway was stuffing a full-fledged falcon into a cage—with a pouch in his calloused hands!

I jumped out and ran before Geoff even had a chance to stop the car. "Let me have that bag!" I demanded as I burst through the entrance. "It's been involved in a crime."

The craftsman looked my way in surprise. His face was leathery and etched with wrinkles. But his eyes displayed a youthful glint.

"So that's why he came home." The shopkeeper spit on the floor in disgust. "I hoped I would be able to sell him again." He held out his hand with the pouch as though resigned to losing both it and the bird.

I slid my gloves on and gingerly took hold of the leather. It wasn't the bag with the diamonds. That was obvious at a glance. But perhaps there'd be some fingerprints. Wishful thinking! There were none, except for a few smudged specimens matching the guitar maker's hands. I was dusting and comparing as my partner sauntered through the door— stooping to keep from cracking his head.

"Can you remember anything," he addressed the proprietor, "about the chap who bought that falcon?"

"¡Chihuahua! What happened to the customers?" The old man straightened out his apron and sat down in disgust at the workbench. "First Mr. Fat starts sprinkling dust around. As if I didn't already have enough! Then you come in with your questions. You want the bird? You can have it. I don't remember anything about the . . . No, I take that back. It was a man . . . with black hair. I told him Flechita was worth fifteen hundred pesos. He offered a thousand. I said I'd accept fourteen hundred. He guessed he could pay twelve—"

"That's all very interesting," Geoff injected. "But half the population of Mexico are men. And ninety-nine percent have black hair. Could you be a little more specific? Was he young or old? Did he have any scars? An unusual accent?"

The proprietor anxiously fingered a thin sheet of mahogany on his workbench.

"All I know," he stated matter-of-factly, "was he had thirteen hundred pesos and knew how to bargain. Not like some of the people who come in here. Hey, what are you doing there?"

He started to get up in protest as I walked calmly into the back room. Weston shook his finger in the gentleman's face to divert his attention.

"What do you have to hide? You aren't perhaps an accomplice to the kidnapping?"

"Kidnapping? Accomplice?" The shopkeeper deflated into the chair. "Surely you don't believe—"

"All I know is that a falcon such as yours carried away the ransom. Are you aware of the penalty for kidnapping and extortion?"

"Penalty?" The man blanched, even under his tan, and swallowed thickly. "I tell you I sold the bird over three months ago. My friends here in town will tell you I am an honest . . . Ask them about Jorge Ortega. They will all say I would not do anything like that. Please believe me, Sargente."

I thoroughly searched the back room and even looked around on the riverbank behind the shop. Jorge had laid up a supply of curing lumber. Squashed tin cans also abounded. But there was no second pouch and there were no jewels. I returned to the shop pretty well convinced of the suspect's innocence.

". . . and if you think of any details," Geoff concluded, "please let us know. Just call the national palace and ask for detective Weston."

"¡El Palacio Nacional! Sí. I will do as you say. What has happened, anyway?"

"We're not at liberty to say," I broke in. "We will be stopping by the police station after we leave here. So please do not make any sudden trips."

"No. Of course not."

Weston looked critically at the falcon.

"We can hardly carry this bird in an open jeep. How much do you want for the cage?"

Jorge's eyes sparkled. "Oh, Sargente, it is a very good cage. I could not possibly let it go for less than six hundred pesos."

My partner scratched his goatee doubtfully. "Some of the bars," he pointed out, "are not very well finished. I'll give you four."

"Oh," Jorge smiled, "but the imperfections show it is handmade. Since you are a respected official, you can have it for five."

"Four-fifty," Geoff decided, "is about as high as I can go. After all, the bird isn't mine. I'll have to drop both off at the crime laboratory."

It was the proprietor's turn. "I understand your problem, Señor. I will hardly make any profit, but you can take it with you for four seventy-five."

"Done," Weston agreed, "if you'll include one of those sombreros over there." He pointed to a table of straw cowboy hats by the wall.

The elderly workman threw up his arms in a shrug.

"What can I do? You will drive me bankrupt, but I agree. They are both yours. Of course, you will also need some food for the bird."

A few moments later we hurried out of the guitar shop carrying the cage between us. Geoff looked ridiculous wearing that hat. In my free hand I clutched a bag of smelly meat scraps and the substitute pouch which, we discovered, contained pebbles. With some relief, we dumped the lot into the rear seat of the jeep. But I eased myself onto the front cushion as gently as possible. Four cramped hours of wild driving had taken their toll. Geoff turned the key and the engine sputtered to life.

"Well," I inquired, "what's your opinion of the man? I believe he told us the truth."

Weston shifted into gear and we started our hunt for the local gaol.

"Actually," he admitted, "I'm inclined to agree. His description of the buyer was so sketchy it's plausible. If he were lying he could have added all kinds of detail. But we will, of course, ask the locals to keep their eyes open."

"After which?"

Geoff smiled as he read my thoughts. He cocked his new hat back on his head like a movie cowboy and affected an American drawl.

"Well now, podnah, ah suppose there'll be time ta eat some grub before we mosey on back."

Chapter 7
The Turned Table

The Inspector's voice on the jeep's radio faded, bellowed, and faded again as we slowed for traffic. Geoff maneuvered past a newspaper boy's overloaded bicycle, then pulled the microphone from its hook and pressed the transmit button.

"Yes, I can make you out, Porfirio. It's too bad you came up empty. But I imagine it would be difficult to track a bird through rush-hour traffic. We're bringing ours home, so if you get hold of a bird trainer, we have a shot at finding the falconer's release point. That is, if the bird remembers. Over."

The radio emitted a loud squawk followed by a wave of static.

"Good news to hear that, amigo But we have big problems. I want you to come at once. Over."

Weston hit the mike button.

"Ten four, old fellow. Tell us the address and as much of the problem as you care to broadcast. Over."

"The address is . . . let me see . . . Can anyone make out a house number from here?" There was another squawk and ocean surf inundated the speaker. Porfirio was busy collecting the information. Crackle . . . squawk . . . hiss . . . "The number is eleven zero six Bernard Shaw Street. Take la Reforma through Chapultepec Forest. Then turn right onto Moliere and make a quick left onto Pátzcuaro. Bernard Shaw is three blocks down. Over."

"I've got that," Geoff responded, "although my guess is he's a good bit farther down than that. What's the commotion? Over."

Whistle . . . squawk . . . hiss . . .

"Claims the person we believe was kidnapped came to his house about an hour ago and abducted his daughter at gunpoint. You-know-who's father is on the way over and the sparks are going to fly. Over."

Weston worked the tuning switch to improve reception. "Who made the claim? We had interference. Over."

Squawk.

"Ruben Rivera, the Minister of Agriculture. I tell you, this case is rolling end over end. We seem to be getting poorer but wiser. You watch. There will be another ransom note in tomorrow's mail. Over and out."

"I wouldn't be at all surprised. Remember your grandchildren! Out."

My partner wore a puzzled frown as he replaced the microphone. My own expression must have mirrored his. I unfolded our well-worn map and began figuring. If we were where I thought we were . . .

"Barring really rotten traffic," I concluded, "we should be there in about forty minutes. Thirty if you follow local custom and don't stop for lights."

"We'll settle for forty," Geoff decided. "I've had enough of local custom for today. When we arrive, let's try to stay in the background and let tempers flare. A good fray can be most revealing."

I tried to coax the map back into a neat rectangle as it flapped in the wind. "What would we say, anyway?" I wondered aloud. "Every theory we had has been demolished."

"Cheeah!" the falcon interjected coldly from his cage. "Cheeah!"

* * * * *

Three-quarters of an hour later our jeep was wending its way up Shaw Street as we searched both sides for house numbers. A tile-roofed Spanish mansion rambled on forever to our left. On the passenger side an oblong flying saucer rested comfortably on a neatly clipped golf-course lawn. A half a block ahead . . .

"There it is," I pointed. "Look at all the motorcars in the driveway. The secret crime isn't so secret anymore."

"Especially," my partner observed, "since several vehicles have press markings on their sides. Rivera must have blown the lid off!"

Our jeep easily navigated the space between stone lion gate posts and muttered its way up the long, horseshoe-shaped driveway. Mr. Rivera was most assuredly a man of means. The house looked like a two-third scale copy of the White House. We pulled up behind the Channel 2 station wagon and strode toward a well-pillared porch besieged by restless reporters. Cameras clicked and whirred and microphones were thrust at our faces as we pushed our way into the melee.

"Is it true the President's son . . ."

"What's your official capacity . . ."

"Can you tell us anything about . . ."

"Will we be allowed in after . . ."

Fortunately, two burly officers battled their way to our rescue and bulldozed through as we shoved and twisted toward the door.

"The Inspector's been waiting for you!" one officer shouted above the clamor. "Just go on in. We'll try to hold them off."

"With pleasure!" I yelled back gratefully.

We managed to open the door a crack, slide inside, and push it closed again against the crush. All of a sudden we were alone in a plush vestibule. Fluffy blue carpet cushioned our feet and wintry Currier and Ives prints decorated the wallpaper. Muffled argument emanated from behind double doors that probably marked the entrance to the living room. We stalked silently over and paused to listen. The fuller, richer of the voices belonged to Augustin. And the deeper . . .

"Of course I opened the door!" Ruben snapped. "How was I to know your son was supposedly kidnapped?"

"If you spent more time at your office—"

"If I locked myself up in that palace, I'd only get one-third the work done. Between the exhaust fumes, coffee breaks, and all that socializing, it's amazing the government even holds together. Don't blame me for not being plugged into the rumor mill! It's your fault this has happened! You and that gangster son of—"

"Gangster! You keep a civil tongue in your head. You know as well as I do there were guns trained on him through the windows."

"All I know is the pistol in his hand was real. And my daughter's gone! I'll see him dead for this if I catch him!"

"It's outbursts like that," Augustin scolded, "that have put you out of the running for the party nomination to succeed me. Get hold of your emotions! We've got to rescue them both."

"You," Ruben fumed, "are an idiot. In the first place I'm not out of the running—no matter how hard you back the Interior Minister. In the second place, you can't face the truth about your greedy, conniving son. Even when he—"

"Greedy! For your information, Salvador helps support two orphanages. When that peasant collapsed on your office doorstep, who was it who paid for implanting a new pacemaker? During the last earthquake, who used his private airplane to fly in relief supplies? Who, Ruben, sent your own family a gift each Christmas!"

"I admit he's a man for grandiose gestures," the gravelly base voice conceded, "but the fact remains he just bled you white with a ransom demand, stole my daughter for some devilish reason, and probably killed that bodyguard as well. Those are hardly the actions of a saint!"

"And those are hardly the doings of my son! You jump to conclusions with such speed—I'm amazed. Spout one more lie to the newspapers, and I swear I'll—"

Geoff swung the doors wide and we marched confidently into the battle. Crystal chandeliers cascaded from the ceiling—their light reflecting from the top of a Steinway concert grand. Chairs and sofas were imported early American. And the carpet hadn't been mowed in weeks. Augustin, Ruben, and Porfirio were all standing—the Inspector apparently serving as referee.

"Gentlemen," my partner declared with authority. "Set aside this petty bickering or both your children may be dead within the week. I have some questions to ask, and I want answers that aren't clouded by anger. Is that understood?"

Ruben Rivera turned in disdain to study us. He was a beardless Santa Claus in a business suit. His chin was double and at the moment he didn't seem the least bit jolly.

"Who the blazes are you two? Not those detectives hired by—"

"The same," Weston cut him off. "But we don't play

sides so far as justice is concerned. Sit down and shut up."

"¡Caramba! I'll do nothing of the—"

"Do what he says," Porfirio commanded levelly. "If we'd followed his advice earlier, your daughter wouldn't be gone now."

The Minister of Agriculture grudgingly slid his bulky frame onto a chair. But he was like a coiled spring ready to snap back up at the drop of a word.

"That's much better," Geoff smiled encouragingly as he pulled over a footstool and squatted like some long-limbed shoe-shine boy. "Now if the rest of you will follow Mr. Rivera's good example, we can get down to business." He waited until we were all seated and looking expectantly in his direction. "Ruben, you begin by telling us in detail what happened."

The official rubbed his fingernails against his lapel.

"With the greatest pleasure. The doorbell rang, so I switched on the intercom and asked who was there. The voice at the gate said he was Salvador Guerrero and had come to visit Zulema. Naturally I was flattered, so I released the lock and hurried in to tell my daughter she had a . . . ahem . . . 'gentleman' visitor. She was practicing something by Brahms on the piano at the time and doing a remarkably—"

"You may," Geoff assured him wryly, "spare some of the details. Did the voice ask if your daughter was home or simply assume so?"

"He never asked," Rivera scowled, "and when the two of us went back to the entrance to greet him, he shoved an automatic in my face, forced me to tie my own girl's hands behind her back, then locked me in the vestibule closet. It took half an hour to get out. I'd still be there if the butler and maid hadn't come home from shopping."

Weston shifted his gaze to the Inspector.

"You have, of course, tested the knob for prints?"

"We have," Porfirio crossed his legs and extracted a notebook from his pocket. "The inside of the door was touched only by Mr. Rivera. The outside bears a couple of clear prints by the maid as well as four made by Salvador's right hand."

"And the outside knob," Geoff inquired, "was it on the

left or right of the door?"

"The right. The frame has been splintered somewhat by Mr. Rivera's efforts to free—"

"I'm afraid I didn't notice it when we came in," Weston interrupted. "How far is the closet from the front wall?"

Robledo pressed his lips together in exasperation.

"Not that it matters, but it's about three meters away, set into the left rear of the vestibule and facing the front entrance."

"Very good," my partner nodded. "An ideal location. You'll notice that if Ruben were walking that way he would hardly be in a position to see the front window. On the other hand, anyone at the window would have a clear shot at Salvador."

"Wait just a moment!" Rivera jumped angrily to his feet. "So this is your unbiased investigation! I'll have you know he could have locked the front door behind him and been perfectly safe standing by the wall."

"Yes," Geoff agreed pleasantly. "And how would any of you have escaped alive? You couldn't have left the wall, you know, without crossing the line of fire. What's more, I imagine steel-tipped bullets would make mincemeat of the door panels."

"Well I . . ."

"In point of fact," Weston observed, "you jolly well owe the young man your life if there were armed cutthroats outside."

"And if there weren't," Ruben added with barely suppressed fury, "I owe him a taste of a firing squad. That man was no more forced to do what he did than you are to be a detective. He actually smiled as I tied the knots."

Geoff pulled a bag of Spanish peanuts from his jacket pocket, tore the wrapper and popped a salty handful into his mouth.

"Oh," he reflected with just a hint of mockery, "how easy it is for a nervous twitch to be misinterpreted. Don't worry about your daughter. We'll have her back safe and sound within a couple of days. Meanwhile, I'd be as silent as a church mouse. Don't say anything that might inflame the abductors. Is that understood?

"Yes, of course."

"Wonderful." My partner turned his attention to Porfirio. "Inspector, there is entirely too much sickness at the palace. And I doubt that exhaust fumes are the sole cause. I want the water tested, the atmosphere examined, and every building within three blocks in every direction searched for transmitting equipment. Some years ago the Russians bombarded an American Embassy with microwaves, and I suspect something similar is happening here. I, for one, do not appreciate having my brains scrambled."

"Nor I," Robledo sputtered. His face registered the same shocked disbelief as the rest of us. "But how could you think such a thing, amigo? We are not a country that indulges in international intrigue."

"I think so," Geoff stated solemnly, "because I've had headaches, John's had headaches, Salvador had headaches, Ruben can't get his work done, and a gentleman with a pacemaker collapsed. Pacemakers are, as you know, affected by microwave radiation. The pattern is too obvious to be ignored. If you catch who's operating the transmitter, it may lead you directly to the kidnappers. A check of power company records should be of some help in your search. If you need to get in touch with me anytime soon, ring Salvador's room at the palace. John and I will be there going over it again. And do turn off the juice as quickly as possible. I find microwaves distracting."

Without waiting for the Inspector's response, Weston turned on his heels and strode purposefully from the room. I shrugged at the others and followed.

* * * * *

Salvador's quarters had aged about fifty years since our last visit. Steel strings protruded from the gutted piano, and furniture stuffing lay like snowdrifts on the rug. The Inspector's men had done an extraordinarily thorough job at searching for the bug. They had, however, neglected to clean up.

"I feel flattered," I commented as we stood in the living room surveying the wreckage. "The locals did a somewhat better job of restoring our apartment."

"No doubt," Geoff noted dryly, "our presence during the procedure made a trifle difference. The prestige of the tenant does not seem to have been the basic issue."

I waded through the mess and bent down to lift the roll-top desk from off its side. "What are we looking for, anyway? I feel rather like an aviation inspector examining the pieces after a crash."

"Fortunately," Weston considered, "I'm primarily interested in the bedroom. And that should still be presentable." He began walking an erratic path in that direction—skirting upended chairs and piles of paper. "But as to what we're trying to find, I'm afraid I haven't the foggiest. Some little thing was wrong in there. Something I probably would have seen instantly if we'd been feeling better. And whatever it is has been eating at me ever since. Even if it didn't register consciously, I sensed it."

"Very good," I remarked laconically as I followed. "We look for something smaller than an elephant and as uncommon as an aardvark. It's good to have the field narrowed down somewhat."

The bedroom was exactly as I remembered. The curtains were open—giving us a view of both a side street and of the square. The mattress lay propped against a wall where I'd left it. And a single dresser drawer was pulled part way out exposing a pile of unused pajamas.

I scanned the art work hanging in the room. "Well," I ventured, "Rouault clown faces on the walls aren't exactly common. Between them, the drugs, and the microwaves (if there are any), it's amazing the chap slept at all. I don't suppose, though, that's the detail you missed."

"Hardly." My partner craned his neck to study the ceiling. "It's eerie, isn't it, to think that even now radiation may be streaming through our bodies."

"Eerie," I disagreed, "is not the word for it. Try infuriating. It's positively obscene for someone to be violating our minds like that!"

Geoff's voice softened as he became philosophical. "We live, John, in a very crowded universe, and I fear we're a good bit less autonomous than we like to think. All kinds of influences impinge on us."

I stepped over to the dresser and began sniffing cologne bottles. "You're right at that," I conceded. "I read once that even bloomin' radio waves in high intensities cause adverse effects. The article listed top floors of skyscrapers as risk areas."

"There are, of course, all kinds of energy waves occupying the same space we do," Weston agreed. "Some beneficial, some harmful. But I was thinking more of spirit beings. We perceive so little of reality, really. Here we humans are, a part of God's creation, literally walking through Him every step of our lives. And being omnipresent He doesn't vacate even a centimeter of space to permit our passage. Instead, He slips through us neatly and cleanly without making contact—unless we've surrendered our hearts to Him. If we have, His spirit intermeshes with ours in an eternal soul shake. Christ is the interface.

"On the other hand, there are demons floating around within the same space occupied by both God and us. The Lord makes no contact with them other than to occasionally restrain their evil machinations. But they can and do influence our lives."

"Only," I corrected, "if someone isn't a Christian. If he is, then the demon passes right through like a radio wave through a receiver tuned to a different frequency."

Weston scrutinized the bed springs with his practiced eye. "I like your analogy," he decided. "It's accurate within limits. But remember that an over-modulated signal can spatter all over the dial. There are harmonic frequencies and—"

"I'm well aware of that," I protested in exasperation. "You're pushing an illustration to—"

"What I'm trying to say," Geoff interrupted, "is that the Christian had better have his tuner right in the center of God's signal to prevent picking up spattering. The longer I live the more I realize that we evangelicals don't take Satan seriously enough. God's spirit intermeshes with ours, but the Lord still *commands* us to be filled with the Spirit, to stop grieving or quenching Him, and to stop giving a beachhead to the devil.

"God, old fellow, is no tyrant. He respects our liberty so much He even allows us to choose to be bad. If we limit the Lord's influence through tolerating certain pet sins in our lives, then as demons float on through they're going to slam-dunk a fair share of evil thoughts into our minds. You're indignant, and rightfully so, about someone trying to manipulate our level of alertness with microwaves. But both of us had better be more indignant, and continually so, about demonic efforts to influence our thinking. It's easy to become spiritually lazy and forget we're at war. It's easy for our soul shake to become limp and unfeeling."

He paused as his gaze passed over the tele. "And I think I've found that little irregularity I was looking for."

"You have?" I snapped closed a box of cufflinks and looked his way in surprise. "What is it?"

Weston gestured toward the face of the set.

"It's strange we should have been talking about zeroing in on the right frequency. The tele is tuned to channel three."

"So?"

"Mexico City, my dear John, does not have a channel three. And the back of the machine isn't hooked up to cable vision, either." He folded his arms and considered the matter. "It is, of course, possible that the billy boys who kidnapped Salvador tried to turn off the set and punched the tuner button by mistake before succeeding, but I rather fancy—"

The bedside telephone jangled and interrupted his thoughts. He pounced on the receiver.

"Bueno. Is that you, Inspector? Yes, we're having a productive time over here. How's your . . . Oh, you have. Did you catch any of . . . They'd already left. What about the equipment? Well, at least they abandoned the heavy stuff. A search of sales records may lead us right to the purchaser. How close were they to the palace anyway? You're joking." Weston cupped his hand over the mouthpiece. "John, go have a look out the side window. I think you're in for a shock."

As he resumed the conversation, I stepped over to the Zapata Street side and gazed out over the roof of the somewhat dog-eared structure across the way. I didn't see a thing. There was certainly no rooftop microwave antenna. The four-story apartment building didn't quite reach to our third level, and it looked almost abandoned—except for wash hanging from some of the window railings. I scanned downward hardly knowing what to expect . . . and discovered Robledo standing in front of a third-floor window waving in my direction and carrying on a conversation over the telephone. I waved in return and he pointed to a large gray dish now pushed back from the opening. It had evidently been camouflaged by some non-flammable screen while in use. I let out a whistle. At this close a range, if the transmitter had any power at all, we were fortunate not to have been killed!

". . . simply can't believe you'd do that. Yes, I know they have the upper hand. Certainly we'll watch. Too bad there isn't a tele over there. Channel five. Of course you may hold on, old chap."

Geoff picked the control box off the night stand and switched on the set. He was right. There wasn't any signal on three—just an indistinct ghost.

"In about thirty seconds," my partner remarked in my direction, "we're going to witness the post-kidnap television debut of Salvador Guerrero. The station received the videotape with instructions to play it sight unseen within five minutes of delivery or both hostages would be shot. The television people called the police, and the police agreed. Let's hope the news people use discretion." He punched the channel five button and turned up the volume.

". . . is impossible to determine beforehand if the President's son made the recording under duress or in a drugged state." The announcer's expression was grim. "But, in the interest of the captives' safety, we now present the tape in its entirety. You be the judge."

The screen went blank for an instant to be replaced by the trim figure of Salvador sitting in an easy chair. His hair was as black and wavy as ever and he wore the same form-fitted suit and flared trousers we'd encountered during our interview. His gaze was penetrating.

"My friends," he began severely, "there are some who will try to convince you that I'm being forced to speak as I will. But I want you to know that that is not the truth. I have left my father's side because I could no longer stomach his corrupt business practices, his acceptance of bribes, and his hatred of you, the people. I have joined with some like-minded comrades and we have begun our campaign of terror against the filthy capitalists who oppress our society." He paused and cracked an amused smile. "We, . . . are on your side. So if there is an occasional abduction, like the one of Miss Rivera, please do not take offense. It's in your best interest. Good-bye for now. Hasta luego."

The screen flickered again and Salvador's fine Spanish features were replaced by the rounder face of the reporter. Geoff switched off the sound and spoke into the telephone.

"Inspector, did you catch what he said? Yes, I agree. Shades of Patricia Hearst. No, didn't look either nervous or drugged. But we'll have to run through the tape a few times to analyze it. John and I will be heading for your office in a few minutes, so if you have the video cassette by then, maybe we can look at it together. I'll also be bringing a most unusual picture that we'll need developed in your laboratory. And while you're at it, arrange for us to use NASA's image enhancer. I believe it's located somewhere in California. We'll link up through a Graphofax machine and ground lines. No, I don't care what Guerrero says. If he wants to see his son again alive, he'll have to agree to accept space administration help. Have a nice day yourself. Ta ta."

Geoff returned the receiver to its cradle and tugged thoughtfully at his goatee.

"What's this?" I inquired, "about a picture? We don't have any that I know of—unless you're going to inundate NASA with clowns."

"Hardly," my friend responded seriously. He punched the control button again and the tele switched to between-station snow. "That is our picture right there. Notice the ghost on the screen. Get a camera from our apartment, old bean, and take your most skillful shots."

"With pleasure, but what am I shooting? It looks like the face of the tube has been burned by someone using a videogame background."

"A videogame," Geoff nodded, "or perhaps a video cassette at stop action. The effect would be the same—an uninterrupted flow of electrons fusing certain areas because there wasn't any image movement to diffuse the heat."

"That's wonderful," I remarked with more than a tinge of irony as I set out toward the door. "We're going to have the National Aeronautics and Space Administration drop everything to find out what kind of games the young man played?"

"Or didn't," my partner called after me.

Chapter 8

The Tele's Vision

This time we walked unmolested through a different entrance to police headquarters. A lift deposited us routinely on the third floor, and we followed the arrows. As we pushed our way into the Criminal Investigation offices, a heightened level of activity was noticeable. Plain-clothes detectives sat at nearly every desk making hurried phone calls and jotting down information. Many were thumbing their way through telephone directories. The whole division had apparently been mobilized to trace the sale of bugs, microwave transmitters, and antenna systems. For the first time I noticed a facsimile printer stationed by the far wall.

Lupe, the charming brunette with the turned-up nose, spied us almost at once and smiled from behind the counter.

"The Inspector is expecting you, gentlemen. Step right on through. He's in his office."

"Thank you." I extracted a film canister from my pocket and handed it to her. "If it's not too much bother, could you trot this on down to the photo lab? The instructions for developing and printing are in the can."

"Why certainly, Señor." Her smile broadened. "Is there anything else?"

"Yes," Weston grinned. "Tell them to hurry. We're in a rush."

"Yes, sir!"

Geoff and I almost collided with the young lady as we passed through the counter's swinging door. She was in a commendable hurry to go out on our errand. While we strode across the office, it crossed my mind that the government could do with more workers of her caliber. Seconds later Weston knocked sharply on the Inspector's glass wall.

"Come in!" The voice behind the pane had a bored lilt to it.

We obliged and found ourselves in semi-darkness. Robledo had his feet propped up on his desk next to a video recorder. He was in his shirt sleeves and watching Salvador's performance on a tele mounted atop a filing cabinet. All that was missing was the popcorn.

" . . . on your side. So if there is an occasional abduction, like the one of Miss Rivera, please . . . "

Porfirio shut off the sound but kept his eyes glued to the picture. He seemed relaxed but far from refreshed after eleven hours on the run.

"Amigos," he declared with a good deal of annoyance, "I have now been through the tape until I'm sick of it. The boy's pupils aren't dilated, and as you say he's completely calm. I'm beginning to suspect Ruben Rivera is right and Guerrero's kidnapping was a hoax." As the recording came to a close, he slammed the rewind button disgustedly.

"Except," I objected, "that the young man would hardly aim microwaves at himself."

Our friend took off his glasses and tried to rub the strain out of tired eyes. "You've got a point there," he admitted. "But maybe others in his gang did it behind his back. Or rays aimed by people unconnected with him may have driven him mad and caused this warped behavior. If so, we're faced with tracking down two sets of traitors instead of one."

Geoff bent across the desk, rewound the cassette, pressed the recorder's play button, and turned to study the screen. Salvador's princely face sprang to life once more.

"Is there anything at all," Weston inquired as we watched, "that has struck you as odd about the mannerisms?"

Robledo forced himself to study the screen again.

"¿Quién sabe? He blinks four times instead of the seven or eight I'd have expected. But he does not show signs of being in a trance. I've had a copy of the audio sent downstairs to be compared against earlier news footage on him. The results reveal identical voice prints. So we are not dealing with a look-alike impostor. Guerrero really did call for the government's overthrow."

"Although," Geoff pointed out, "he was obviously reading from a teleprompter."

Porfirio threw up his hands.

"So he's got a rotten memory! The words are what count, not his style of delivery. And . . . "

The telephone on his desk clanged raucously. Seemingly relieved at not having to sit through another showing, the Inspector made a grab for it, leaned far back and stuck the receiver to his ear.

"Bueno . . . Oh, it's you, Mr. President. Yes, we have been. I'm afraid though that . . . You have! That at least offers some encouragement, although I don't know what Weston has in mind. Thank you very much for calling. Adiós."

He hung up and paused to digest the information.

"Augustin Guerrero," he informed us solemnly, "has just had a conversation with the President of the United States. You *have* your access to NASA's image enhancer— whatever it is. For Augustin's sake, I hope you know what you're doing. His expectations are far too high considering the circumstances. And an international incident just may result from the request."

My partner hit the rewind button for yet another run through the tape. But his movement was nonchalant— seemingly unconcerned. "You needn't worry about an incident," he drawled. "An image enhancer wouldn't be considered a spy device by anyone—unless perchance he resided on Mars or Venus. Simply stated, it's a computer that reconstructs weak and garbled signals from deep space. The thing blots out 'snow' and other garbage, erases echo images, sharpens the focus, and connects together broken lines. That's all."

"And what do you propose?"

"Oh," Geoff smiled brightly, "I would very much like to know what picture the electron gun on Salvador's tele has burned into its tube."

Porfirio slapped his forehead so hard it must have stung. "You can't be serious! You've involved two governments in order to find out channel eleven's test pattern?"

"That, of course, is a possibility," Weston agreed good-naturedly. "But I rather fancy Guerrero dozes watching channel three."

"Which," the Inspector declared, "is just as bad. If you

look at my set, you'll see it's on the very same channel. Video recorders use either that or four, and four is occupied by a broadcast station. The young man probably stopped the action on a movie, left to answer the door, and forgot to return until the damage had been done. NASA will really be tickled when they produce a scene from Las Calles de San Francisco."

"I imagine they would be," Weston agreed, "if they did. But they won't."

"You're sure?"

"Absolutely." Geoff stuck a finger in the air for emphasis. "For one thing, there's no indication in Salvador's room that he ever owned such a recorder. If he did, he kept it a secret and took it with him. I asked around the palace. Secondly, a man of his stature would have hardly tolerated a bad picture tube indefinitely. So I conclude the ghost was recently burned. In my opinion the image on that screen may go a long way toward establishing the chap's state of mind at the time of his disappearance. The case is essentially solved, but the additional evidence may help insure a conviction."

Robledo shook his head incredulously.

"If you mean by that that Salvador is guilty, then—"

"I mean neither more nor less than I said," Weston snapped. "Tomorrow morning at seven I want every available suspect or witness to meet with me in Ruben's living room. At that time I'll expose the full dimensions of the plot. Later this evening you'll be getting a list of those whose presence is required."

"My partner," I assured the Inspector, "has not gone bonkers from the microwaves. He's his usual melodramatic self, so I suggest you comply with the demand no matter how outrageous it seems."

Porfirio looked from one to the other of us as though trying to somehow assess our motives. For a split second I didn't know whether he would explode in exasperation or burst out laughing at our lunacy. Instead he simply shrugged.

"I said when we first met," he reflected in a voice bordering on a whisper, "that you were folk heroes. When one invites a Joan of Arc or Pancho Villa to help, I suppose one must learn to accept the unusual."

"Since I neither hear voices nor rob travelers," Geoff smiled, "I'm not sure I see the connection. But your cooperation is very much appreciated. Say, you haven't come up with a trace on any of the loose hardware we've been stumbling across, have you?"

"Not thus far. We know who sold the eavesdropping device, but the salesman says a street urchin bought it for cash. The youngster was probably paid a few pesos for the errand."

"Speaking of which . . . " I glanced down at my watch. "We should be getting delivery on our photographs by now. The desk clerk ran them down to your laboratory."

Porfirio stretched, then lifted himself out of the chair.

"In that case," he declared as he slid into his jacket, "let's go into the outer office and make sure the communications link with the computer is set up. We might as well know as soon as possible whether we have candy or switches in our stocking."

"More than likely," Weston amended, "it's rat poison."

I took the rear as the Inspector led us out into the nerve center of his crime-fighting empire. As we walked between desk rows he asked the detectives for progress reports. Each in turn did his best:

"Sorry, sir, I've about finished with the electronics bodegas, and none of the warehouses indicates—"

"A search of the area hasn't as yet turned up the young boy. Perhaps they brought him in from another colonia. We're expanding the search to include—"

"Inspector, I'm about ready to beat my head against the wall. One distributor is double checking his inventory. He thinks he's missing some—"

"No trucking company has a record of having delivered the equipment to—"

"We've found the electrical workers who installed the new wiring, but they can't remember—"

"Señor, the lab boys report there were no prints at all on, in or around the transmitter. The entire room looked like it had been steam cleaned, and—"

"We're still trying to determine what spy devices were removed and when. A shopkeeper says he saw some workers loading boxes on a truck yesterday. And today just before we arrived a couple of men came down the stairs carrying some kind of 'radios.' But the old gentleman didn't get a good look at either the workers or. . . . ''

We approached the facsimile machine, more sober, but very little wiser. The revolutionaries we were up against seemed to be an extremely professional lot! The apparatus before us reminded me of a sleek, full-sized photo copier. It was, however, far more than that. Working on the principle of the television camera, it reduced pictures to electronic impulses for transmission through telephone lines. It could also receive and reconstruct photos transmitted. A curly haired technician was stooping at its side to make last minute adjustments. Porfirio patted him on the back like a father greeting his son.

"¿Juan, cómo van los preparativos? Has the switchboard been contacted by the Americans yet?"

The intense younger man twisted a final set screw and straightened up in the presence of his superior.

"They have, sir, and we're about ready. I sent off a picture a few seconds ago to test the line. When they return it, we will find out if there are any interference problems. Everything on this end seems to be—"

"¡Señor Weston!"

The brunette was out of breath as she burst through the door. Judging from the perspiration on her blue uniform, she had literally run the whole way.

"I've got . . . I've got . . . " She slowed self-consciously to a fast walk as she crossed the busy room. " . . . those photographs you ordered. It took . . . a little bit longer because the matte finish paper was . . . at the bottom of a pile."

There was a hissing behind us as microjets sprayed ink onto a copy sheet. The technician scooped up the finished transmission almost at the same time that Geoff extended his arm for the woman's envelope.

"Eleven by fourteen," she explained, as she handed over the package, "is a little larger than we usually . . . "

"I realize that," my partner agreed. "Thank you ever so much for your effort." He turned to the technician, who was examining the transmitted copy with a magnifying glass. "Is the connection good?"

The expert flipped the magnifier back into its plastic case and returned it to his pocket.

"Not just good," he declared with satisfaction, "it's perfect. If you'll let me have those photos before conditions change."

"Certainly."

Weston quickly released his prize, and the policeman fed snapshot after snapshot into the jaws of the contraption. We'd exposed a whole roll while varying exposure time, brightness, and screen contrast in hopes of capturing every last shred of detail. Finally the last eleven by fourteen slid from sight, and all we could do was wait.

"I must congratulate you two," Porfirio commented dryly, "on your thoroughness. I've never seen so many shades of fuzzy."

"When we go off on a tangent," I snickered, "we go all the way."

"Why, of course. You're the ones who see behind mere physical appearances. As a matter of fact, I've continued reading beyond the chapter you recommended, and I have to admit that—"

Ink began spraying onto the copy sheet, and we gathered around to watch the results. Before our eyes a black and white portrait quickly took shape. First there was a wall, then the top of a window, the tip of the Latin American Tower in the distance, raven hair waving peek-a-boo across a forehead, penciled eyebrows, large round eyes, a gentle nose, a small, unsmiling china-doll mouth over a rounded chin, an ancient rooftop across the street behind her head, the straight-backed chair she sat on, slender, crossed legs, an electrical outlet, baseboards.

"Blimey!" I breathed. "Didn't I see a picture of that woman on an end table in Ruben's?"

"You certainly did," the Inspector confirmed grimly. "It's Rivera's daughter. No wonder Salvador took the recorder with him. He must have been obsessed with her—hiding his passion and clandestinely preparing to take her prisoner. The treacherous dog! Well, my friends, now you know your client's state of mind. I, for one, am glad I'm not employed to help him."

"You and I both," Geoff concurred. "May I have this photo for the evening? I'll bring it with me without fail to tomorrow's meeting."

Porfirio lifted the sheet high and presented it ceremoniously to him.

"With my compliments for a masterful piece of detection. You've dexterously slid a noose around a deserving neck."

"One man's noose," my partner declared as he folded the evidence and slid it into his jacket, "is another's escape rope. Add faith to your intellect, Robledo, and you'll be a smashing detective. We'll see you at first light tomorrow."

My partner and I shook his hand perfunctorily and then strode purposefully toward the exit. Geoff was in such a hurry that he broke into a run once we reached the hallway. I had all I could do to keep up as we sped around corners in a race for the lift.

"Why on earth the rush?" I lunged at the last second and made it through closing doors. "You'd think there was a fire!"

"There is," Weston agreed with sober urgency, "and it's going down. I have less than an hour's daylight left for buying surveying equipment and putting it to use. If I don't, we're risking another murder."

"Don't worry, old bean," I encouraged. "We should make it if the location isn't too distant."

Weston gazed at me steadily. " 'I,' John, not 'we.' There may be some bloke following us, and if there is I want you to lead him right back to the palace. I jump from the motorcar at the tube station entrance. Is that understood?"

"Perfectly. And if the Inspector calls?"

"Tell him you haven't the foggiest where I am. It's absolutely critical that no one knows what I'm about."

"That should be easy enough," I complained, "since even I don't know."

"Good," Weston concluded, "let's keep it that way. But if I don't come back, think 'face plate.' "

The doors slid open, and we continued in a near trot toward the entrance and the street beyond.

"This is disgusting," I muttered just loud enough to be heard. "It's bad enough we have a client who writes riddles about shadows. Now my own partner has caught the disease!"

* * * * *

By the time I returned to the National Palace and had had supper delivered by a caterer, the sun shining through the bedroom doorway was merely a dull glow on the horizon. As I sat at the table munching frijoles, enchiladas and tacos, I talked to the Lord about the case and about my friend out facing danger somewhere. After perhaps fifteen minutes, my sense of urgency lifted, and I was flooded with calm. I realized that my prayers were answered. The remainder of the meal was given over to thanking God for His love and faithfulness.

One of the nice things about paper cups and plates is that, once used, they can be tossed into the dust bin and forgotten. So the cleanup was done in two shakes, and I settled down on the sofa for a relaxing evening studying through the parables. My thinking was clearer than it had been in several days, and I was impressed by Christ's brilliance in confusing His enemies and teaching His followers with the very same stories. Fiction seemed to me such an effective tool for communicating truth. . . . I wondered in passing why so few Christian writers today followed Jesus' example. As I was about to turn the page, there was a resounding knock on the door. Even before getting to my feet, I knew instinctively there was a starched uniform out on the walkway. Only a bobby or a soldier would employ such rat-tat-tat precision. It turned out I was right on both counts. The door swung open to reveal a poker-faced member of the Policía Militar. What was a surprise, though, was his female companion bundled up in a knee-length coat and with a pocketbook hanging from her shoulder.

"Señor," the guard informed me in an energetic monotone, "this joven told us at the entrance that she wanted to speak with you. Do you wish to be bothered?"

I noticed the steady seriousness in Maria de Jesus' expression as she stood with half her face obscured by shadows.

"It won't be any bother at all," I assured him. "You are to be commended, Sergeant, for bringing her up. If you have time, wait outside the door for a few moments, and you'll be able to provide her a return escort."

The man's jaw seemed nearly immobilized by his helmet's tight chin strap.

"Yes sir. Will that be all, sir?"

"Quite. Thank you." I turned to my guest. "Miss Ayala, do come in. It's your house for what it's worth."

She attempted a smile and glided past me as I closed the door. Her dirty-blond hair, though carefully combed, hung limp. Earrings dangled like wind chimes from both lobes. This meeting was obviously of some importance to her.

"May I help you off with your wrap?" I offered. "It gets a mite nippy around here after sundown, doesn't it? Perhaps a spot of tea?"

She stood for me to remove the coat. "Gracias pero no, Señor. This is not, strictly speaking, a social visit."

"I quite understand." I folded her garment and laid it across an end table. "Have a seat and we'll get right down to business. That easy chair over there is particularly comfortable. The police managed to return the stuffing to approximately the right places. You don't mind if I have a cup, do you? It's an old British custom, you know, like the Changing of the Guard and flies in summer."

"Not at all." Maria's lips parted in genuine amusement. "We have at least one custom in common, anyway."

My young visitor waited patiently while I poured the brew and plopped in a single lump. But . . . Maybe it was my imagination or the golden glint I'd noticed in the back of her mouth when she smiled. She looked like someone steeling herself for the dentist's drill. I carried cup and saucer to the sofa, made a soft landing, and gazed her way expectantly.

"Señor Taylor," she began with a somewhat nervous forcefulness, "I have just been given a police summons to appear at some kind of meeting. They told me if I had any questions I could come here and talk to you or your companion. And there is a question. Will you . . . Are you going to . . . "

"Expose you?" I raised my eyebrows. "Frankly, it's Geoff's show, and I haven't an inkling of what he's planning."

She gestured imploringly with her hands. "But you

mustn't! Please tell him not to. It would simply kill my father if he found out. My whole life would be ruined."

I took a sip of tea and looked at her steadily over the rim of the cup. "Maria, if it's at all possible to keep your drug abuse out of tomorrow's discussion, you have my word that Geoff will do it—on one condition. Stop taking the stuff, and present us with medical evidence for the next twelve months showing you're not cheating. Otherwise, we'd be doing you a favor by uncovering the boil so it can be lanced. I won't protect your hypocrisy and see you dead of an overdose in two or three years. Nor will I cover up continued criminal activity."

The girl blinked rapidly, clasped her hands, and studied her intertwined fingers before returning my gaze. Her voice was high pitched—almost childlike.

"I'd like to lie to you," she admitted haltingly, "but I guess it wouldn't do any good. I appreciate your offer, too. The truth is I don't know . . . if I can stop. What Mr. Weston said yesterday scared me, and I decided then to say adiós to pills. But when I did, they didn't want to go. Everything round I saw—buttons, light bulbs, even the moon— called to me to swallow pretty, round tablets."

"And did you?"

"Yes . . . Just like some addict. I even prayed, but it didn't do any good."

I nodded in a mixture of sympathy and satisfaction.

"That's all very encouraging, Miss Ayala. I'm glad to hear you say so."

Her gray eyes widened. My response was clearly unexpected.

"But I thought . . . "

"That I'd be shocked? Or filled with pity?" I took another sip and set the cup down on the sofa arm. "Actually your candor is a refreshing change. Now that you've shed some of your rationalizations and are willing to admit what you are, maybe some good can be accomplished."

Maria bit off a hangnail and looked at me uncertainly.

"You're talking about religion again, aren't you? Between you, your friend, and that sister of Salvador's, I'm literally surrounded by 'hallelujahs.' "

"If that term," I replied, "is a religious slur, then I plead guilty. So, I presume, would Handel, since he wrote *The Messiah*. But doesn't it say something about you that you consider the thought 'praise the Lord' an aberration? Any expression can be emptied of content through overuse, of course, but that's hardly reason to—"

"Oh, I'm sorry." Her words came out with a rush. "I didn't mean to offend you. Honestly, I didn't. I think I just envy you for having your life under control. If I could stop taking drugs, perhaps I'd become a . . . an evangelical, too."

"That's like saying," I pointed out, "that if you could flap your arms and fly, you'd consider becoming a bird. In the first place, your featherless efforts would be unlikely to succeed in putting anything but your friends to flight. In the second, you'd lay an egg at laying eggs. One does not try to be good enough to become a Christian. One becomes a Christian, and the Lord provides the ability to be good. He may also rap you soundly across the knuckles if you stubbornly decide to hang on to a habit or two."

Maria paused to turn the matter over in her mind.

"I don't know," she decided softly, "if I could live up to being one."

"Why," I disagreed with a tinge of sarcasm, "of course you could. By your own efforts you could emulate all the disciples. Peter cursed and denied Christ three times. John Mark abandoned Paul in time of need. Diotrephes was a conceited prima donna. Barnabas was carried away by Peter's hypocrisy and refused to eat with the Gentiles. Ananias and Sapphira were struck dead for greedy lies. They were all the same miserable failures you are whenever they tried to live on their own strength.

"Can't you get it through your head that I'm not talking about 'works righteousness'? I'm talking about a God who loved you so much He sent His Son to be your proxy on a cross and pay for *all* your sins in a crucible of blood, sweat, and agony. I'm talking about Jesus Christ offering you a free gift, if you'd stop spitting in His face long enough to receive it. I'm talking—"

"I would never spit in—"

"Oh, yes, you would. You have, and you are. Jesus says 'I am the way.' But you reject His whole reason for coming to earth, try to wheedle through His earthly mother, storm the gates of heaven with drug highs and now even consider earning your passage by your own laughable goodness. There's only one way you'll make it, young lady, and that's by giving up on yourself and surrendering your heart and life to Jesus. Are you disgusted by your sinfulness enough to really want His pardon, knowing that when you receive it He'll come into your being and make all kinds of changes?"

Maria sat staring at me for a long time. Her peasant blouse rose and fell with her deep breathing. A quivering lower lip betrayed her intensity.

"Yes," she decided at length," I . . . think I am. What do I do?"

I sighed.

"You trust. You entrust yourself. You receive. It's as simple as that. I suppose I could lead you phrase by phrase through a litany, but then the prayer might seem like just another prescribed work. People call on God by mouth, by sign language, or even through pantomime. But in all cases it's the heart that matters—not the outward expression. Why don't you pray silently and I'll do the same."

She nodded her assent and we knelt down on the tile floor. With closed eyes we each talked to the Lord. I could hear Miss Ayala whispering softly as I poured out my sincere request for her salvation. I pled with God, asking that He'd produce real repentance and trust within her. And I fervently hoped that she wasn't just going through the motions to keep from being exposed tomorrow. When I finished and looked up, I saw tears streaming down her cheeks as she continued her heavenly conversation. I knew then that somewhere angels were rejoicing. Moments passed and all that could be heard was the hum of an electric wall clock in the kitchen and the rumble of an occasional heavy truck on the street below. When my guest opened her eyes and sniffed back the tears, she was radiant.

"I never knew," she whispered in a voice near laughter, "that prayer could be so beautiful. I feel like . . . like a new person."

"More importantly," I rejoiced with her, "you are one. And that makes all the difference."

Maria got to her feet, picked her pocketbook off the chair, and rummaged through it. Her hand emerged holding a prescription bottle which she extended toward me.

"Here, Mr. Taylor, you take these. I won't be needing them anymore."

"With pleasure." I slid the pills into my pocket. "After you leave, they'll find their way into the sewer where they belong. Before you go, though, I would be remiss if I didn't share some advice with you about living your new life."

My guest settled back into her chair with a bounce and looked my way with youthful exuberance.

"¡Maravilloso! I would love that. Start with lesson one, 'maestro.'"

I couldn't resist grinning. She was suddenly so transparently enthusiastic. In answer, I stepped over to the telephone table, brought back the city directory, and started thumbing through it.

"The first thing you should do," I advised, "is to buy a Bible and other Christian literature and start reading voraciously. I personally like works by C. S. Lewis, Luis Palau, and John Montgomery, but there are a whole host of good books. Read the New Testament first, then the Old, then branch out to contemporary authors. Ah, here it is. There's a Christian bookstore nearby that should be of help. La Puerta de la Fe over on Carranza Street. They'll be able to suggest some good Bible study tools. I'm afraid I'm not up on what's available in Spanish."

"That," Maria observed, "sounds easy enough. I've always loved reading. What's next?"

"Next," I suggested, "find an evangelical church and make it part of your life. Paloma can help you there. Perhaps you two might attend together. But if you don't feel you fit in with that congregation, seek out another where the people are both sensitive to your daily needs and pray for you as you fight your battles. There may also be a Christian coffee house in the city that will take the place of some of the night spots you're used to visiting."

She nodded her head in agreement and leaned slightly forward.

"And," I continued, "keep your eyes on Jesus. Satan will marshall his forces against you now that you've chosen freedom. I can almost describe his tactics in advance. He'll send friends your way with drug offers. The moon will be just as round as ever and even more reminiscent of tablets. Your non-Christian relatives will accuse you of craziness and of betraying the family religion. School will become so demanding you'll have little time for prayer and Scripture study. Satan will cause the more carnal of your Christian acquaintances to disappoint or embarrass you. And to top things off, he'll try to entice you with so-called 'little' sins. Once you give in to them, the Holy Spirit's protective influence over you will lessen and you'll be powerless to resist the 'biggies.' "

Maria bit her lip at the dismal picture. Her enthusiasm was still there, but tempered with the realization of the frightful war which lay before her.

"You," she decided, "don't sugar coat anything you say, do you? How can I survive under those conditions? Go out in the desert and be a hermit?"

"Hardly," I chuckled. "But there are a few rules of thumb you might find helpful. First, don't let sins pile up. If you do something wrong, ask God's pardon immediately. Second, face temptation with prayer. Don't just say no to the pills. Concentrate your thoughts on Christ. Third, if your love, joy, peace, patience or self-control start slipping, look for sin in your life and confess it to the Lord. Those fruits of the Spirit will be in you unless you're hindering Him. Last, discover your spiritual abilities and put them to practical use. Don't be an 'average' Christian mouthing words and playing pointless games. You can't afford that. Read the last half of Luke chapter seven and apply it to yourself. You've been forgiven an awful lot. Love Christ more than others do.

"That's about everything I can say except that God promised He won't let you be tempted above your ability to resist. You have a struggle ahead of you, but it will be a glorious adventure. You're in God's family now, and He won't let you down."

My guest smoothed the folds of her dress. As she considered my words, her face assumed its characteristic French pout. But her eyes sparkled. "I feel clean inside, Mr. Taylor. No, I *am* clean inside. And I want to stay that way. I appreciate what you've said. I think a lot of it was from your own experience, wasn't it? And I'll heed your warnings. May I call you to ask for prayer if I start to weaken?"

"You may," I invited, "as long as I'm here. But long distance to London costs a pretty penny. Talk to Paloma. She may just be available. Remember, though, I still want that monthly medical report."

Miss Ayala's lips parted into a broad smile as she stood up and retrieved her coat.

"Señor Taylor, your words are so blunt. It's easy to see you're not a Latin. But even when you try to sound gruff, I can see that your heart is gentle. I *will* live for Jesus, and you will receive your reports. Thank you for everything you've done." She held out her hand. "I had better go now. There are still studies to do and I've got to be you-know-where early in the morning."

I scrambled to my feet and enclosed her slim fingers in a beefy handshake.

"I quite understand. We'll see you in a few hours, then. And hopefully Salvador's return will follow shortly thereafter."

I insisted on helping Maria into her coat and accompanied her as far as the door. There the soldier took over escort duties and led the way around the courtyard toward the stairs. After waving a final farewell, I hurried into the bathroom on an errand. I no doubt killed ten sewer rats with a single flush.

The rest of the evening was spent in praying for Maria, studying more parables, and watching the tele. The cartoon version of *The Lion, the Witch and the Wardrobe* was featured on the educational channel and I found the Spanish dubbing every whit as stimulating as the English original. When the show ended, I decided to call it a night. The image on the screen shrank instantly to a white dot that itself began to fade.

I switched off all but one reading lamp and started off toward the bedroom. Before I'd gone half the distance, however, the front door sprang open and Weston came sauntering through whistling "The Blue Danube." I hardly recognized him. His sports jacket had been replaced by a collegiate sweater, his hair was cropped short and his goatee was missing! He'd also managed to pick up a cassette recorder during his travels.

"What in the world," I demanded, "happened to you? You look like a sheared sheep!"

Geoff tossed the recorder onto the nearest chair and grinned broadly. "John," he enthused, "you would have given your eye teeth to see it. I was followed all the way to the Latin American Tower by some blighter with a bulging coat. He stayed outside while I carried my transit to the observation deck. When I was through up there, I abandoned the transit, bought some new clothes in one of the building's shops, got a haircut and shave, and walked right past the chap at the front entrance. He didn't know me from the man in the moon. Never criticize my goatee, old fellow. It allows me to occasionally disguise myself as me!"

I rolled my eyes in mock despair. "Oh, bother! Do you mean you're going to let it grow back? The finished goatee isn't bad, but the initial stubble causes clients to cringe."

"Clients," my partner assured me as he felt his chin for emerging hair, "are a hearty lot. They'll survive. And they're primarily interested in results, don't you think? I can tell you the Guerreros will see a few tomorrow. We needn't worry about any rubber-hose confessions in this case. We're going to expose one of the most dastardly plots in the annals of crime."

"That's gratifying," I drawled, knowing full well he wasn't going to supply any details. "You'll never guess who dropped by while you were out on the town. . . . "

Chapter 9

That's Showdown Biz

The falling mist swept the air clean of traffic fumes, but it also coated the streets with a slick sheen. Two crumpled fenders had to be pried apart up ahead, and by the time our motorcar reached Chapultepec Forest we were already running a quarter-hour late.

I tuned across the radio dial and hit upon an English-language station playing tinny Jelly Roll Morton records, interspersed with advertisements for the Folkloric Ballet. The combination was incongruous to say the least. Once again we turned onto Moliere and then followed Pátzcuaro to Shaw Street with its lineup of stately mansions. In spite of the rain, two hearty maids were out for their ritualistic sweeping of sidewalks. Seconds later Geoff braked and steered the jeep up into the driveway.

No press vehicles were visible this morning, but their absence was more than offset by ranks of black limousines and two-tone police cruisers lining the drive. We pulled up boldly in front of the portico, slammed motorcar doors, and walked past a contingent of Robledo's regulars. Geoff took the lead while I carried a briefcase stuffed with potentially decisive evidence. Without a word the two of us entered the house and padded across thick carpet toward the waiting assembly. The living room, when we arrived, was its same grandiose self, sporting hotel-lobby opulence, a brick fireplace, and enough crystal hanging from the ceiling to imitate a hailstorm. The tempest struck as we walked through the entrance.

"There are the lousy finks!" Shaggy jumped up from his spot on the right-hand sofa between the black giant and

Moonstone. He lunged toward us with foaming hatred in his eyes, but tripped on his leg irons and fell flat on his face. In utter frustration he banged his cuffed fists against the green pile of the carpet. "You bummers on wheels! You slimy, slick-tongued liars! If I ever get my hands on you!"

Two uniformed officers peeled off from their positions near the wall and thrust the struggling hippy back to his seat. As every eye was on the spectacle, I took the opportunity to study our guests.

Pet was in a straight-backed chair—her chain tied securely around one of its legs. The girl's mousy hair was even more matted than before, but her eyes and nose weren't running, and she seemed relatively calm. To her left, Maria de Jesus, Paloma and Augustin leaned forward on a sofa. Farther over, an easy chair sagged under Ruben. He seemed bored by the stupidity of the interruption, and impatient to get things moving.

Folding chairs had been brought out for the rest of the guests and lined up in a neat row—completing the left leg of the horseshoe. A gentleman who looked to be Memo's father was seated on the end. Next to him two palace guards shifted uncomfortably, Salvador's chauffeur yearned for a steering wheel, and Rivera's maid perched with all the animation of the Sphinx.

Porfirio stepped over toward us with his arm extended. "Compadres, it's good to see you again. I could hardly sleep last night waiting for this moment. I see you have acclimated yourselves well to Latin time, no?

I returned his handshake heartily. "If you mean by that," I ventured, "that we're almost half an hour late, I plead guilty."

Robledo moved on to enclose Geoff's hand in a Mexican "soul" grip. "No," he asserted, "I do not mean that at all. We just got some of your more bizarre witnesses settled down. I must say I don't know what to do with them after we're through here. They got to the toilet before we could break the door down, but from the very smell of the place—"

"I know," Weston nodded, "they're on drugs. Personally, I'd recommend drying them out for deportation to the United States. There may be warrants out on the hairy one. He appears to be rather violent."

"That would be . . ." Porfirio consulted a notebook. "James Duncan. As a matter of fact, they've all overstayed their six-month visas, so I don't—"

"What's that you're jabbering about me in wetback language, you stinking pigs?"

"Why, Jim," my partner smiled, "you're remarkably responsive today. I see you recognize your own name. But don't you think it's you who are the wetbelly?"

Shaggy started to get up again, but his black companion pulled him down.

"Shove it, man. You're digging our graves with your big mouth. Be cool, and—"

"Be cool," Jim spat with the vehemence of an aroused cat. "Be cool, after those dudes chased off nearly all our chicks with their cheap trick! Be cool, when they fingered us and had us brought—"

"Silencio!" Ruben's shout almost rattled the chandeliers. He bounced to his feet and pointed his stubby arms at the hippies. "This is my house, and I want order. It's disgusting enough you're even here. Shut your slimy mouths so we can get this inquisition over with!"

The two hippies looked at each other in bewilderment.

"What," Jim asked mockingly, "did he say?"

"He said," Augustin translated dryly from across the room, "that he has a crocodile pit in the backyard and he's going to feed you all to them if you make another smart remark."

Shaggy blanched behind his beard and bit his lip. Mexican law was an unknown quantity to him, and he must have heard some lurid stories. As Ruben returned slowly to his seat, Porfirio took command of the gathering.

"Ladies and gentlemen," he began in melodic but firm tones, "there has been a series of crimes committed, as I'm sure you're all well aware." He paused briefly to clear his throat. "Mr. Weston has been cooperating with us in the investigation and now feels he knows who the guilty party or parties are. So I want your undivided attention as we turn matters over to him. Be completely open, as any evasiveness on your part will count heavily against you. Mr. Weston . . ." Robledo gestured for my partner to take over and then deposited himself on an empty folding chair.

"Thank you, Inspector." Weston stepped to the center and addressed the gathering. "I will attempt to expedite matters in accord with Mr. Rivera's wishes. John, will you please drag a table this way and set up the valise."

"Gladly."

I pulled in a bar stool that would serve nicely, set the briefcase on it, and opened the lid in such a way that it shielded the contents from the gathering. While I was doing so, Geoff continued with the preliminaries.

"We are," he remarked conversationally, "a rather heterogeneous mixture, and it will occasionally be necessary for me to change languages while speaking with different people. For the few who are bilingual, that will pose no problem, but I apologize in advance to the rest." He paused to repeat the statement in English for the benefit of the hippies. Weston was not particularly dignified as he stood barefaced and clad in slacks and a sweater, but his eyes had a certain hawkishness about them. Not a whisper could be heard above his translation.

"Now," he concluded, "let's get down to cases. In every crime there are two essential ingredients—motive and opportunity. We'll examine motive first, since on the surface it seems by far the easier to fathom. One hundred million pesos is, after all, a fairly tidy sum to accrue through a single kidnapping. But what of the other abduction and the murder?" He gazed down the row of chairs to the wrinkle-cheeked office worker on the end. "You, Mr. Hernandez, certainly had ample reason to strike your son dead. He was—"

"Me!" The man seemed stunned. "Why, I loved him! He was my oldest boy, and . . . "

Weston extended his hand for silence. "And," my partner continued, "he was both neglecting the family and taking drugs. You knew the former and must have suspected the latter. You may even have wrongly concluded that Salvador was his supplier."

"So that's why," Porfirio broke in, "we have these hippies present. I'll have an autopsy performed to check for . . . "

"My Memo, he was a good boy!" Hernandez stood up and shook his finger toward Porfirio. "You bury him, do you hear? I don't want any knife cutting him up!"

Geoff stared calmly at the father.

"Sit down," he commanded levelly, "and let me finish. I'm not making accusations—yet."

The sprightly gentleman looked at us uncertainly, then returned with poor grace to his chair.

"Thank you." My partner bowed slightly in appreciation. "Now as I was saying . . . You get off work a little earlier than your son. You could have arranged a meeting with him, knocked him on the head in anger, disposed of the body, and driven to within a couple blocks of your house. That would account for Memo's assailant being in the back seat. He trusted you. It would also supply a motive other than money for selecting Salvador as a victim. But there are, of course, problems with the theory. Given Memo's temper, you might have brought a rock with you for protection. But you don't smoke, and it's probable the killer does. What's more, your boy's body wasn't dumped into the pond until after the motorcar was abandoned and the park closed. You don't own a motorcar, do you?"

"No," Hernandez replied emphatically. "I take the metro."

"That much," Geoff smiled good-naturedly, "seemed obvious. The only private vehicles out front are a mite beyond your income bracket, and we're over a mile from the nearest tube station. You didn't drive because you couldn't. Nor, for that matter, could you have disposed of the corpse without an accomplice who owned transportation. As for kidnapping Salvador, even the possibility was beyond your means. If you'd squeezed out every bit of information on the palace defenses that Memo possessed, you still would have been powerless. That effectively eliminates you as a suspect. I invited you here to see the young man's murderer exposed."

Relief flickered across Hernandez' face only to be replaced by irritation. "You've got an awful way," he growled bitterly, "of doing someone a favor."

"Not at all," Geoff denied as he started pacing. "I simply illustrated the point that virtually no one in this room is above suspicion. The killer had better start worrying. You guards . . . " He gestured toward the two palace soldiers. "You check the boots of incoming motorcars. Did anyone examine the luggage compartment of Salvador's limousine when it was driven out the day following his kidnapping?"

There was an embarrassed silence.

"I thought not." Geoff looked sternly from one to the other of them. "But it *was* gone that afternoon."

"I . . . " The chauffeur cleared his throat and looked extremely uncomfortable. Pigeon English forgotten, he reverted to Castilian. "I took it out for periodic maintenance. But honestly, there could not have been anything in the trunk. We opened it when we rotated the tires."

"Which," Weston continued, "precludes Salvador's using the boot without your knowledge. Of course you might have consciously aided him in making an escape. But I'm not totally satisfied with the theory." His manner softened. "The parking lot, you see, is awfully close to the front entrance. If the door were opened for an incoming motorcar, the limousine would be spotlighted for the outside guards. The insiders would be even more likely to notice activity right in center courtyard. And if you and Salvador had conspired, that still wouldn't tie in the microwave setup next door."

Geoff shifted his attention from the Aztec face of the chauffeur, past both Ruben's chair and the inscrutable eyes of the President.

"Miss Ayala," he beamed, "you—like the others—have a motive of sorts. Salvador had rejected you, and revenge might have been sweet. But you had neither opportunity to act nor reason for participating in the related crimes. You are, therefore, here primarily as a witness." Geoff started to stroke his absent goatee but caught himself in time.

"Paloma tells me she doubts her brother could be forced against his will to speak. You've been in a position to observe him over a period of time. Would you concur with that estimate?"

Maria shifted in the sofa and pushed a stray lock of hair back behind her shoulder.

"Yes," she asserted seriously, "I would. I was with Salvador out in the desert once when two scorpions stung him. He killed them both, smashed their nests, and gritted his teeth as he drove home. He wouldn't even let me take the wheel. A man like that would not give in to threat or torture." She looked about her as if seeking support. "I don't care what people say or what they think they saw, he wouldn't. And he never would have said those awful lies about his father. He respected Augustin more than any other man on earth!"

"Well, he said them!" Ruben pressed a handkerchief to his bulbous nose and blew. "Unless the man has a double, he's a loathsome scoundrel."

My partner nodded thoughtfully. "We do have a considerable difference of opinion here, don't we? But I'm certain matters will resolve themselves."

He switched to English and spoke in rapid, clipped tones to the hippy leader. "Did you ever see a small-mouthed, black-haired girl in the company of Memo or his friends?"

James, taken by surprise, scratched his pock-marked cheek at the beard line. "Who, me?"

"Yes, you."

"Naw." He stuck his thumb in his girlfriend's face. "That is, except for Moonstone here. Sometimes she'd be the cat's guide when he tripped. You know, to keep him from running into meteors or getting lost out in space. But I'm only saying that to help you out, see. And 'cause I know these pigs here don't speak English. I ain't gonna make no admission in court that we been usin.' "

"Yeah, mister," his belly-buttoned companion echoed. She pulled up her legs to squat Indian-fashion on the cushion. "That Hernandez was a real neat guy. Kinda square, but nice."

Weston smiled. "Thank you very much, young lady. If you had answered those questions a couple of days ago, perhaps we could have dispensed with your presence." He fixed her with a penetrating stare. "Remember my advice to your group?"

Moonstone met his gaze without flinching.

"I will," she admitted firmly, "but it won't do no good. I belong to Jimmy, and we're going to go to hell together."

"I see." My partner shook his head ever so slightly. "It's your choice, of course, but I hope you change your mind. Love doesn't exactly bloom in a heated frying pan."

"We'll be praying for you," I interjected. "And—"

"I wanta go home," Pet whined from her chair. "This

place is such a bummer. Harsh . . . It's harsh, and I've gotta think too much. I wanna dream and float and . . . Did you know the sky is pink? And purple eyeballs drink a pint of vodka with a single breath. I studied to be a brain surgeon. If you need an operation, come to me and I'll give you a special price. If you untie me, I'll play the piano for you. . . . "

"Little girl," I asked pityingly, "where's your home?"

"704 Marigold Street in Houston. Hey, you're trying to trick me." She kissed her chain and rubbed it affectionately against her cheek. "I live right here in Mexico City. And we don't take any drugs at our commune. I wanna go back *there*!"

I ignored her glare and jotted down the numbers. By this time the English-speaking members of the group were looking with horror at the wreckage of a mind. Even those who understood only Spanish realized something was wrong.

"I have a house," Maria offered. "If they let you stay in Mexico . . . "

"Buzz off, sister!" James shook shackled fists in defiance. "What is this, some kind of conspiracy to break up a family? She's happy, so leave her alone."

"Happiness," I retaliated, "is a state of mind. And her mind's in a pretty foul state. So 'buzz off' yourself. Whatever happens we'll see you don't get either brain or body, you filthy—"

"¡Caballeros!" Ruben thundered. "I don't know what this is all about, but I'm certainly not here to watch some stupid argument over a lunatic. Either get on with this farce or get out of my house!"

Weston's jaw set.

"Indeed," he declared quietly, "we will get on with it. Let me start by revealing how the central crime was committed. No, it wasn't some far-out hippy scheme. It was cold-blooded, calculated and devilish. Far more sinister than anything our 'lunatic' friends here do in their most crazed or demon-controlled moments." He paused to take a sheet of copy paper from the briefcase, unfolded it, and held it up for all to see. "This picture was burned into the screen of the television set in Salvador's bedroom. Mr. Rivera, do you always jump like that at the sight of your daughter?"

"I do," the portly statesman responded indignantly,

"when some man keeps her photo in his room to ogle it."

"How interesting," Geoff mused. "The Inspector 'jumped' to the same conclusion. But it's quite wrong, I assure you. Salvador had no home video machine. Did you know," he addressed the group with a wave of his hand, "that it's quite possible to hypnotize a chap in his sleep? I won't fill in the details lest you try it yourself, but I assure you it can be done."

"That's all very interesting," Porfirio observed, "but I don't see what it has to do with—"

"It has everything to do with it," Weston shot back. "Look at the physical evidence. What do we have? A transmitting device under the bed . . . A transmitter on the other side of the street . . . And a tele that can be activated by remote control. Put that together and you've got a good sight more than bibbity-bobbity-boo."

"By George," I exclaimed, "you don't mean that Salvador was hypnotized from across the street?"

"Most certainly," Geoff confirmed. "The bug in the living room assured the mind-stealers that he was alone in the apartment. The—excuse the expression—bed bug enabled them to hear the young man's responses to their commands. And a remote unit similar to the one on Salvador's night table turned the tele on and off and switched it to the channel on which they were broadcasting. I imagine the volume began low so as not to wake him and picked up after they gained control. The television transmitter and slide camera were obviously a part of the equipment removed from the microwave site before our arrival."

"But this is preposterous!" Ruben objected openmouthed. "Why would anyone use my daughter's picture that way? If you're insinuating that she was somehow involved and *ordered* Salvador to kidnap her, you're madder than that . . . thing over on the easy chair."

"I'm insinuating nothing," Weston assured him pleasantly. "I'm merely stating facts. Little by little somebody took over Guerrero's sleeping moments. Probably after a while a single trigger word was sufficient to put him into a highly suggestible state. Then one night he was ordered to leave the palace in search of the girl he'd been commanded to love."

Maria gasped. "Then you mean . . . "

"That's right," Geoff declared grimly. "He was probably fed a pack of falsehoods about you to poison his thinking so he'd drop you without doing violence to his will. The will, you see, can be violated through hypnosis by simply altering one's perception. If, for example, I set a man in front of a television camera and give him a post-hypnotic suggestion that he's an actor trying out for the part of a guerrilla leader, when he awakes he will look at the teleprompter (as I've commanded) and read his lines *with feeling*."

"¡Caramba! So that's how it was done!" Porfirio waved his arms like an excited orchestra leader. "That explains the number of blinks. He was trying to obey the command *literally* by looking without interruption!"

"Obviously," Weston agreed. "But just as one can slow a heartbeat through hypnosis but can't stop it, neither was the involuntary blinking response completely eliminated. Salvador didn't seem in a trance because he was acting a prearranged part, and his own will was circumvented since he could see nothing wrong with playing a distasteful theatrical role."

Ruben Rivera got slowly to his feet. His thick lips were twisted into a sneer.

"You can talk all you want to about only dealing in facts," he charged icily, "but it sounds to me like you're pointing the finger at Zulema. Sticking a bundle of lies together to save Salvador's precious neck! She's no ringleader, and you'll never prove otherwise!"

"Sit down," my partner demanded with carefully controlled firmness. "Your daughter's no ringleader, and I'll never accuse her of being one."

"I'll stand, thank you."

"Very well then, stand—where you are. Why in the world do you want to be president, Mr. Rivera? You seem to have so much trouble keeping your temper in check."

"To serve the people," Ruben fumed. "To speed progress . . . To improve oil drilling efficiency . . . What kind of question is that, to ask in a criminal investigation?"

Geoff brushed aside the question and pulled the ever-present bag of peanuts from his pocket.

"The human mind," he observed as he tore open the

wrapper, "is a man's real castle. His entire future—all of eternity—depends on the decision of his will. Calvinists may stress God's sovereignty and Arminians the human response, but neither conceives man as a mere humanoid, manipulated by some capricious puppet master. God, my dear Rivera, is a *gentleman*. He calls, He draws, He sends human witnesses, He shapes circumstances to teach us our need for Him, and then He knocks on the door of our castle. He doesn't bash it down with an atomic fist or slip in through the keyhole and stage a coup. From His point of view He's sovereign. From ours, we're free to choose or reject."

"Are you a raving psychotic?" Ruben slapped his thighs in utter consternation. "My daughter is *missing*. Can't you get that through your skinny head? We don't need a sermon. We need a solution!"

With infuriating sluggishness, Weston poured peanuts into his mouth and set about chewing. As he did, he studied Rivera, from his alligator shoes and extra-large, tailored suit, to his bull neck, heavy eyelids, and neatly combed hair.

"Why," he wondered aloud, "do you have to out-god God?"

"What!"

"Even those hippies over there," my partner gestured with his thumb, "are as much victim as villain. Each undermines the other and is in turn undermined. But you . . . " Geoff's voice took on sledge-hammer force. "You manipulate and even kill to obtain power. Then you have the gall to claim you want to 'serve' the people! The devil himself couldn't—"

"That's a lie!"

Before we could stop him, Rivera was all over Geoffrey with his fists flying. He caught my partner with a wild roundhouse that almost floored him. Then he followed with a left to the stomach. Weston ducked desperately to avoid another ham-like blow, then countered with two quick jabs and a karate punch to the chin. The Minister of Agriculture fell like a sack of flour. While he lay moaning on the floor, Porfirio bent over and slapped a pair of cuffs on him.

"Thank you," Weston managed as he fought to catch his

breath. "As . . . I . . . was saying. God is a . . . gentleman. I should . . . have expected . . . less polished manners . . . from a killer. Stuff him back . . . in his seat and I'll provide . . . your proof."

"Why not," Robledo concurred grimly. "He looks undignified there on the rug. Samuel, Antonio, come give the man a lift."

Two uniformed officers circled from behind the piano and approached the fallen politician with guns drawn. They searched him for weapons, then bore his weight between them and plopped him unceremoniously on his chair.

"I can't believe it," Augustin declared as he, along with everyone else, sat down again. "He's certainly an opportunist, but a murderer?"

"I *am* not," Rivera groaned as his head wobbled from side to side. His eyelids opened, and he tried to focus. "Can't you see he provoked me to fight . . . to make me look bad?"

"Well," Porfirio nodded, "he has surely succeeded in that. Sit still and listen. If you feel Mr. Weston is manipulating evidence, say so *civilly*. Do you understand? Otherwise we'll throw you in jail for assault right now and go on without you."

Ruben finally focused on the Inspector.

"I understand," he promised haltingly.

"Wonderful," Geoff enthused as he felt a tender spot by his eye. "That should speed matters up nicely. I would like to apply an ice pack in time to keep the swelling down.

"Let me see, now where was I? Oh yes . . . If you'll look carefully at the photograph of Zulema, you'll notice that the electrical outlet on the wall has an unusual face plate." He retrieved the paper from the floor where it had fallen during the scuffle and pointed to a spot next to her leg. "It's rather fancy, isn't it—with curves and swirls . . . The plate that is. Porfirio, if you reexamine the tele footage on Guerrero, you'll find a nearly identical cover on a light switch. I conclude, therefore, that the picture of Zulema—which we were never intended to see—had been taken in the very same building where Salvador was being secreted. Notice the background in Zulema's photo. There's an old rooftop nearby tilting slightly in the wrong direction. That in itself isn't uncommon. Many buildings around here are a bit tipsy from earthquakes. But the Latin American Tower in the distance provided an additional key. Most ancient structures in the city aren't over five or six stories high, so that was the base from which I computed. Using the photograph I estimated east-west lie and also the angle of incline to the top of the tower. I then climbed the skyscraper with a surveyor's transit, paid my twenty pesos to get onto the observation deck, and reversed the process. What should I see as I angled down but a leaning church with the top floor of a hotel peeking over its roof. So I trotted on over and had a look."

"And why," Porfirio demanded, "didn't you bring the police along on your junket?"

"Because," Geoff pointed out, "you were convinced of Salvador's guilt. And I was just as certain that at the first hint of police discovery Zulema would jolly well blow the man's head off and claim she'd overpowered her captor. That was the beauty of their scheme. Zulema disappeared as a supposed victim so she'd have an excuse for, as it were, getting rid of the evidence.

"The name of the hotel, incidentally, is The Diligence. I paid for a room, climbed to the roof, and lowered a microphone to the top of what I believed the right window. The decorations on the edge of the church roof proved useful in guiding me. The mike picked up a woman inside playing 'alacrán' with two men, neither of whom was Salvador. I was able to get a clear recording for about half an hour. Then it got chilly enough so one of them closed the window. Would you all like to hear a sample?"

"No," Ruben snarled, "we wouldn't. You had no legal authority to bug the room."

"But Señor," Robledo smiled impishly, "he did not bug the room. He bugged the air outside the room. And that is public property."

"What's more," Augustin snapped, "you're interested in letting the *facts* be known, aren't you Ruben?"

Rivera's only answer was a sullen, expressionless stare. So my partner removed a cassette recorder from the briefcase and pressed the play button. The girl's voice was crystalline, lilting, and syrupy.

". . . calavera. One more, and I win. You know I'll really be sorry when I ask him to open his mouth wide so I can stick the barrel in. He's such a sweet boy, really. And I've always wanted to own a slave. I guess the important thing is he won't feel any pain. Oh my, I win again. This is my lucky night."

Geoff punched the stop button. I shuddered and noticed my loathing mirrored on the faces of everyone who understood Spanish—except for one whose heavy lids narrowed to slits.

"If that's my daughter," Rivera declared in a strained, higher pitched voice, "then she acted on her own. She's an adult. She has a bank account. I don't know all her friends."

"So," Weston smirked contemptuously, "parental love finally grows cold. I was wondering when desire for self-preservation would take over. Do you really expect us to believe that your daughter hypnotized Salvador so expertly that he walked into your house and successfully faked a kidnapping? Or that she had enough money to buy all the electronic paraphernalia we've found lying around?" Geoff reached into the briefcase again and exhibited a plastic pouch. "Frankly, I don't know if it was you or Zulema that left this Fiesta cigarette ash at the murder scene." He tossed it back into the valise. "But I know you've made enough mistakes to put you in front of a firing squad."

"Such as?"

"Such as," my partner obliged, "ringing up your stooges after we left here yesterday, so they could grab broadcasting equipment and run. There were only five people who knew we were aware of the microwave nest. John, Porfirio, Augustin, you, and I. That narrowed the field down a mite, didn't it? Neither John nor I had tipped off the operators. That left three. And only one of the three was always conveniently absent from work while his fellow governmental leaders were exposed to daily radiation.

"You made another mistake in the way you orchestrated Salvador's mysterious disappearance. Oh, yes, I know how he got out of the palace. He used the escape tunnel—the only unguarded exit. He didn't know the door combination, did he? But he was taught it over the tele. Now who in this room do you suppose had high enough rank to possess the combination? Augustin, certainly. But he had everything to lose from the kidnapping. Who else? Only *you*. You told Zulema, she told Salvador, and out he walked.

"I think, though, your worst blunder—and most stupid—was having your daughter order Salvador to open the closet door without specifying which hand to use. Being right-handed, he naturally gripped with the right in much the same way he hefted a letter opener the night we met him."

The fat man had taken on a hunted look. Perspiration beaded on his neck, and his breathing was coming fast and heavy. "What of it?" he rasped. "He was right-handed. He used his right hand. You're talking nonsense!"

For the first time my partner viewed the suspect with a degree of compassion.

"I do hope," Weston declared softly, "that you put your trust in Christ before they execute you, Ruben. Even actions as evil as yours can be forgiven."

"Answer my question!" Rivera demanded. "I don't want any more of your religious garbage. What about the hands?"

My partner's gaze hardened to flint. "Very well. I'll try to make it simple. A left-hung door at the left corner of a rear wall could be entered only from the right. One would therefore expect Salvador to hold his gun on you with his right hand, open the door with his left, and usher you in. If he gripped the knob with his right as the prints show, he would have had to shove his pistol under his right armpit to keep you covered. And that stretches probability to the breaking point. You're a dead man, Rivera. Perhaps if you help us free Salvador, they'll let you off with life."

The Minister of Agriculture gasped, rolled his eyes . . . and fainted. His chin fell forward—almost disappearing in a roll of fat. The hands that had nearly felled Weston hung uselessly behind his back. I looked on the pitiful sight and wondered if it would be his shoes or Zulema's that were embedded with seeds from Carbonera Street. The case was closed.

Epilogue

Later that afternoon Geoff and I dined in style with Maria, Paloma, Augustin, and the Inspector on the Latin American Tower's forty-second floor. Hanging plants provided greenery, and table-top-to-ceiling windows afforded a breathtaking panorama of the city. A waiter had just presented us a flaming shish kabob, and my knife was gliding effortlessly through a filet mignon.

"It's gratifying," I remarked to no one in particular, "that we were able to rescue Salvador without bloodshed, even though he must remain under observation for a few days. I'd call this case a definite success."

"There's no denying that," Maria agreed seriously, "but I'm still not sure why Rivera engineered the kidnapping in the first place or why he and his 'lovely' daughter killed poor Memo."

Porfirio sipped a cup of steaming hot coffee. "As to the murder," he considered, "Hernandez must have discovered or been on the verge of discovering the microwave center. They elected to silence him."

"And," Paloma commented between bites, "one hundred million pesos was a lot of money even to a man like Rivera."

"Yes it was," Weston agreed. "But there was far more to it than that. This whole thing, as nearly as I can tell, was a grand design to wrest the presidential candidacy of the PRI party from the man Augustin was backing. The microwaves were intended to create an inept government. Salvador's television appearance would discredit your father. And the ransom money was probably ticketed for paying bribes in the convention. You all would have been bankrolling your own defeat."

Augustin wiped gravy off his mustache with a napkin, then shook his head in wonder. "What a fiendishly clever plot! And it would have worked, too—except for you. You handled Ruben magnificently, Señor Weston. By the time you'd finished with him, he was so terrified he turned over the jewels without blinking, and practically led the charge on Zulema's apartment." The President switched to English so Porfirio wouldn't understand. "I'm also grateful you kept Salvador's unsavory conduct out of it. Rest assured, it's at an end."

"I'm sure it is," Geoff responded in the same language. "And there wasn't any evidence against him anyway, since the witnesses weren't about to admit their own involvement. All that could have come from the revelation was harm—to you, to him, to Maria."

"¡Oiga!" Porfirio complained. "What are you two doing? Passing on secrets?"

"Certainly," Weston grinned as he stuck his fork into a sweet potato. "And that's what they'll remain. Secrets."

Maria tossed her blonde cascade back over her shoulders and reached for a glass of milk.

"Can anything be done, Mr. President, about my helping that unfortunate hippy girl?"

"Since," Augustin observed, "her mother told us over the phone to 'drop dead,' I can't see there'd be much point in sending her home. But you can't attend school and nurse an addict at the same time. I won't consider arranging what you want unless you agree to two conditions."

Her face fell. "I'm afraid to ask. What are they?"

"Paloma and I have discussed the situation at length," Augustin hedged, "so perhaps she should be the one to—"

"Stop it, Daddy," Paloma laughed. "You're going to give her a heart attack. Maria, he says that if I bring one of the family maids along, I can stay at your place a month or two and help out. We can study the Bible and pray together and talk to the hippy. What's her name, Daddy?"

"Melany."

"We can talk to Melany about our faith and about how to become clean. That is if you'll let me come over."

"Will I let you!" Maria almost jumped out of her chair for excitement, and my nose came close to being skewered by her fork. "You bet I will! It's the best thing that could ever happen to me!" She calmed down to mere exuberance. "Thanks, Paloma, from the bottom of my heart. And to you, too, Señor Guerrero."

Augustin shrugged, but there was the glint of delight in his eyes. "It is nothing. But be careful."

Porfirio reached over for a roll and started buttering. "I hate for us to get serious again," he apologized, "but there's one thing, Geoff, that still bothers me. In Rivera's living room you said that everyone present was a suspect. Did that include me?"

"You're a good detective," Weston smiled. "You should know it did. After all, you agreed to televise that infamous tape. And you could have tipped off those chaps in the transmitting center just as easily as Ruben did. I wasn't sure of your innocence until you allowed me to take Zulema's picture along with me. You didn't recognize its tremendous import."

"Saved by my ignorance," Robledo mused. "That's not very comforting to my ego."

"But then," Weston chuckled, "ego is a creature that needs very little comforting. And the salvation that matters most in this world doesn't depend on wisdom or merit. Paloma and I will be going on a date this evening. If it's all right with her, why don't you toddle along as chaperone and we can discuss some spiritual realities?"

The President's daughter gazed at my partner through deep brown eyes. "I have a better suggestion," she offered with a coy smile. "Let's talk to Mr. Robledo right now. I doubt that he would enjoy the ballet."